To Connie,
Many blessings,
Pat

Prov. 3:5-6

The Good Path

Pat Nelson Klud

WestBow
PRESS
A DIVISION OF THOMAS NELSON
& ZONDERVAN

Copyright © 2016 Pat Nelson Klud.

All rights reserved. No part of this book may be used or reproduced by any means, graphic, electronic, or mechanical, including photocopying, recording, taping or by any information storage retrieval system without the written permission of the author except in the case of brief quotations embodied in critical articles and reviews.

WestBow Press books may be ordered through booksellers or by contacting:

WestBow Press
A Division of Thomas Nelson & Zondervan
1663 Liberty Drive
Bloomington, IN 47403
www.westbowpress.com
1 (866) 928-1240

Because of the dynamic nature of the Internet, any web addresses or links contained in this book may have changed since publication and may no longer be valid. The views expressed in this work are solely those of the author and do not necessarily reflect the views of the publisher, and the publisher hereby disclaims any responsibility for them.

Any people depicted in stock imagery provided by Thinkstock are models, and such images are being used for illustrative purposes only. Certain stock imagery © Thinkstock.

Scripture taken from the New King James Version. Copyright © 1979, 1980, 1982 by Thomas Nelson, Inc. Used by permission. All rights reserved.

ISBN: 978-1-5127-5412-4 (sc)
ISBN: 978-1-5127-5413-1 (hc)
ISBN: 978-1-5127-5411-7 (e)

Library of Congress Control Number: 2016913569

Print information available on the last page.

WestBow Press rev. date: 09/19/2016

Foreword

Once again, the author has taken suspense, romance, the element of surprise, the depravity of man, and the love and redemption of Christ, and pulled them all together to encourage, entertain and convict. *The Good Path* was delightful. I enjoy linking the characters from each of the previous encounters, *Green Glass* and *To Fill A Home*, and seeing what amazing things God does in their lives while marveling at how the power of prayer looms throughout the pages.

Minister Paulette Holloway, MSW, LICSW
Ministerial Staff - All Nations Baptist Church,
Washington, DC
Executive Director, Phyllis Wheatley YWCA
Author, <u>Tea With God – Everyday Encounters</u> and <u>Thieves of Intimacy</u>

Acknowledgements

First of all, my grateful thanks to those of you who have read my first two novels, *Green Glass* and *To Fill A Home*. Your kind comments and recommendations have been most encouraging.

Abundant thanks also go to my faithful readers and reviewers: Paulette Holloway and Robin Gailliot, whose comments, advice, proofing, editing and encouragement were priceless. My dear husband, Leon, is my biggest fan and editor. Without all their input, there would be many more mistakes and incomplete thoughts.

Above all else, I thank God for His inspiration for this and every story. No matter what we go through, there is always assurance of His goodness and forgiveness. He can and does make a way where there seems to be no way.

Enjoy!

You will show me the path of life, in Your presence is fullness of joy; at Your right hand are pleasures forevermore. Psalm 16:11.

Chapter 1

Roberto Jenks descended the courthouse steps with a smirk on his face. His highly-paid lawyer once again had gotten him off without even a warning. Even though he was on trial for murder—huge bribes and intimidation had won him another victory.

So what if he had ordered the demise of two people? The witnesses who had been paid to swear to his innocence had been so believable! And the judge, threatened by a scandal over his secret affinity, kept him in his place.

Reminding himself to reward his attorney with a box of his favorite cigars, Roberto got into the sleek limo awaiting him at the curb.

"Where to, boss?" asked his faithful driver, Jackson.

"Home, James," said Roberto, laughing. It was a standing joke between them.

As the black car pulled away from the curb, Roberto reached for the phone in the console beside him.

"Hi, it's me. I'm on my way home." After a few more minutes of conversation, he replaced the phone and settled back into the plush leather seat. This was the way to live!

What a waste of time this whole trial business had been. There wasn't anything concrete to tie him to the murders. One of his bodyguards, Tiny, had let it slip to the police detective that he had acted on Roberto's orders. Nothing came of it. Roberto had made sure that. Too bad. Tiny was a faithful foil. There must have been something in what he ate to cause him to just keel over like that. Ha!

Arriving at his upscale apartment building, Roberto exited the limo and told Jackson that he would not need him anymore that day. He entered the building, put his keycard into the elevator slot, and entered the glass-enclosed conveyance. Reaching his own domain, he removed his suit coat, and headed for the well-stocked liquor cabinet along the wall of the living room. He needed a drink, now.

Leaning his head back against the cushions of the luxurious leather sofa, he relaxed for the first time in weeks. Mr. Big was not going to give him many more chances like this. He'd better be more discriminating in the future when he made sure of the removal of his adversaries.

Closing his eyes, he fell into a dream of terror. He saw flames and heard wailing, but he couldn't find his way out. The phone ringing beside him brought him to with a start. Sweat ran down his back as he reached for the instrument before the sound could rub his raw nerves any more.

"Yeah?" he bellowed into the mouthpiece.

"Is that any way to talk to your bread and butter?"

Sitting up as if he'd been caught stealing from his mother's purse, Roberto answered, "Sorry, I must have fallen asleep. The phone woke me up."

"So, you're out of trouble now. Don't think I intend to give you any more slack. You were sloppy in your handling of your business. You can be replaced, you know."

"Yes, sir," Roberto said with trepidation. He did not want to find himself on the bad side of his superior.

"Do you think you can handle the next piece of business I have for you?"

"Anything you say, sir. I'm your man," he said with more bravado than he felt.

The controlled voice on the other end outlined his next assignment. Roberto listened like a man getting instructions for buried treasure. He wasn't about to miss anything important.

"Have you got all that?"

"Yes, sir! I won't let you down."

"I'm counting on you, Roberto. This business depends on employees who can do their jobs and keep their mouths shut. You need to guarantee that those who carry out your instructions understand this. No more slip-ups. You understand?"

Roberto heard the unspoken warning. Assuring his employer of his ability to handle his mission, he hung up with a sigh of relief.

How did he get himself in so deep? He only wanted to make money and live comfortably. When had he gone from a small-time crook to a big-time villain? He was so indebted to that guy; he'd never be able to get extricated.

Shaking his head at his traitorous thinking, Roberto made up his mind to stick with it for now. Soon he would have enough money to skip the country with his nest egg, never to be heard from again. At least that was the way he wanted to disappear. Not like so many others who had turned up missing. Not wanting to even go there in his thinking, he went to the bar and poured himself another drink.

It was time to put the ball into motion.

★ ★ ★

Fellow Rosemont police detectives Todd Chambers and Kirk Walters found themselves faced with a list of unsolved cases that seemed to be never ending.

Kirk mused out loud, "How is it that we can have so many crimes and so few convictions? Will you look at this list?

Murders, robberies, stolen goods. When will it end?" he added in exasperation.

Todd nodded his agreement. "I believe we are both good detectives. It's just that the criminals seem to be getting smarter. It's not that we are unable to do our jobs. When slick operators like Roberto Jenks have enough money to buy him an acquittal, what are we supposed to do? He was as guilty as sin."

"I agree. One of these days, he's going to make a mistake that even he can't escape. I can't help believing that he works for someone else. I don't think he has the brains to carry out all the things that seem to point to him," replied Kirk.

"Yeah, I think you're right about that. Roberto is a pawn for someone else. But who? That person's identity is so well-hidden in the machinations of these crimes, he's hard to pinpoint," Todd said, agreeing.

"I can't help believing that if we pray more and complain less, someone will slip up. I thought for sure we had Jenks set for a conviction. But our star witness disappeared. Someone must have paid big for his freedom. I would love to get my hands on the brains behind this operation. He really must be the top man on the totem pole if Jenks works under him."

Todd pushed the list aside and leaned back in his chair. Without another word, the two men bowed their heads and took the matter to God—the only One Who has all the answers.

Following their impromptu prayer session, Kirk got up and left Todd's office to finish some paperwork on a case that had just been completed. At least with that one, the criminal had confessed. Some things did work out for the good.

Todd mused over Kirk's attitude. It hadn't been that long ago when his friend and co-worker wanted to quit the police force out of frustration. But with his new commitment to faith and prayer, and with Todd's encouragement, Kirk had realized he was right where God wanted him.

Without divine direction and assistance, this job would make any man want to give up. It could be so frustrating at times, especially when people like Roberto Jenks, who were obviously guilty, got off scot free. Todd reminded himself—again—that God is the keeper of the books. He knows the thoughts and actions of each person. Only He can bring justice in the end. That gave Todd the assurance he needed to keep working diligently at his job, catching criminals and trying to see that they paid for their crimes. He would have to leave the rest to the Lord.

Chapter 2

It was an early autumn day, warm, bright, and sunny, without a cloud in the sky, as day God had ordered especially as a send-off for the future.

Time couldn't pass quickly enough! This was the day! In just a short while, eight years of Randy Burnett's life would be but a dark memory. Serving time in prison had not been all that terrible; at least that's what he had told his mom, Sally. But today, he was going home!

Sally uttered a huge sigh of relief as she pulled into the prison parking lot. No more of this dreary place for her boy. Boy? He was now thirty-four, with his faith still intact and growing. She thanked God often for that. All her prayers and those of her friends kept him on the straight and narrow during his years of confinement.

She waited outside the main entrance, just as Randy had instructed. His release was scheduled for ten in the morning. Only a few minutes more to wait!

Butterflies fluttered about inside her as she stood waiting in anticipation. Only God knew what was ahead. All she could focus on for now was his coming home.

Soon, the huge gate opened. Out walked a smiling Randy. He grabbed his mom and swung her around in a circle.

"I've never felt so free in my life," he said. "Except when I gave my life to the Lord," he added.

"You look great, son. I'm so happy right now I think I could burst. We may not know what's ahead, but we do know the One Who knows."

"You got that right!" he said as he walked to her car with his arm around his mom.

On the way home, Sally asked him what his plans were now that he was a free man.

"First thing, I have to get my driver's license renewed; and then I need to check in with my parole officer. He'll be setting up my hours of community service for the foreseeable future.

"The warden gave me the name of a bakery owner who might be willing to take me on as an apprentice," he continued. "When I was given the choice of working in the machine shop or the kitchen, there was no contest! Greasy hands did not appeal to me at all! Flour-covered hands, however, didn't bother me one bit. I found out that I liked it," he said as he eased himself into the comfortable passenger seat of his mom's car.

"There's a satisfaction that fulfills something deep inside me when I make something good out of simple ingredients. I can't even put a finger on why. I didn't even know that desire existed," confessed the newly-released young man.

"I'm sure that wherever you put your hand to, you will prosper. There's a Bible verse to that effect."

"I love that about you, always including scripture in our conversations. It seems so natural. I want to be like that now that I don't have to watch everything that comes out of my mouth," replied Randy.

She answered back, "I just know what I've learned over the years of study and practice. The Word works. That's all I can tell you."

"Yes, I've seen that happen on more than one occasion. Let's hope and pray that I can be as bold and confident in my life," Randy responded thoughtfully.

The rest of the way home, they talked about the new things they were learning from scripture, and all the blessings they had received.

Relating to one another on an adult level had made them friends as well as mother and son. Sally prayed that they would never lose that special attachment. It was even better than anything she had imagined.

Sally had been praying for her son for so long, ever since he left home at seventeen. Through those years when she had no idea where he was, she could only pray and believe that he was safe and well.

When he finally made contact, but told her virtually nothing about his life since leaving home, she had been so overjoyed to see him that she didn't want to make him leave again by asking too many questions. She was content to feed him a Sunday dinner occasionally and have a less-than-informative conversation. Just having him home for a meal was enough at that time.

She learned later that Randy never knew the true identity of his last 'employer.' The truth had finally come to light, and he was arrested shortly thereafter. When the police officers arrested Randy at Sally's home that Sunday afternoon, she couldn't believe their charges, especially when Randy didn't deny them.

His confession of faith that very morning at church couldn't have come at a better time.

Finding Tom Burwell, a lawyer from her church, had been a godsend. Randy was a first-time offender, and had returned much of what he had taken. Therefore, the lawyer helped to get his sentence reduced. Only eight years' incarceration had been issued instead of a much longer sentence for a more hardened criminal.

But, all of that was behind them now as Sally drove them home. She wondered what life would hold next.

★ ★ ★

Randy began talking with his mom about his life since he left home at seventeen, having been convinced that he didn't need to finish high school. "At the time, I had no idea what the 'real' world would be like.

"Unfortunately, that freedom wasn't as exciting or satisfying as I'd thought it would be. But I was too proud to go home and admit that I had made a terrible mistake.

"After Dad died when I was young, I could never seem to get my bearings. Some new friends at school pulled me away from the standards of my upbringing until I didn't know who I was or why I was here. But I was persuaded to think that I knew how to take care of myself without anyone else telling me what to do! It seemed like my new friends were enjoying the freedom of leading their own lives—minus the rules their parents had taught them.

"Oh, how wrong I was. Little did I know I would end up on the streets, which proved that was not the best place to live. Menial jobs were all I could get since I didn't get that little 'piece of paper' called a diploma!"

It was as if a dam had burst and his story could no longer be held back.

"When I was approached by the *Boss*, making money was all I could envision. I convinced myself that the thieving I did was okay because I never hurt anyone. I was simply doing my job and helping myself up the ladder. How clueless and naive I was to imagine I would never be caught and have to pay the price with years of my life.

"Now that I'm a free man, and already got my GED, getting an honest job will not be as difficult as it had been without one."

Sally let Randy share all that was on his heart. She was so grateful to hear him unashamedly tell her of his struggles, she didn't interrupt with questions. There would be time for those later.

Randy continued, "Ever since committing my life to the Lord, there was no question in my mind about Who is directing my life. Instead of jumping at everything that comes my way, I will now willingly wait for divine guidance.

"Getting to work in the prison kitchen was God-directed. The cook, Marcel, was a former head chef at one of the best restaurants in his community. Getting greedy had sent him to prison for some 'readjusted' thinking. In the meantime, he tried to fix meals and desserts that reflected his own personality. Most of the other prisoners just ate what was set before them, not realizing how fortunate they were to have a guy of his caliber serving them.

"I recognized right away that Marcel's approach to meals was more than just doing his job of feeding a bunch of hungry men. The meals were healthy, had variety, and were also appealing to the eye. Of course, the bare necessities were all that he was given to use, but he made the best of them."

Taking a long swallow of water from a bottle Sally provided, he went on with his thoughts, "Along the way, I took an interest in Marcel's recipes, especially those for the desserts. When we weren't busy mixing, chopping, stirring, or seasoning, we had time to bring to bear the creative ideas that Marcel held in his memory. Baking had been his forte in his previous life, so he wanted to pass on to me everything he knew in order to help me have a new start when I was able to leave this 'fine establishment,' as he called it. And I am grateful to him.

"I hope I have learned enough to be hired. I'm looking forward to meeting Mr. Foster, whose name and address were given to me by the warden. If this is in God's plan, then I have nothing to fear. If not, then I know that something better awaits me."

Finally able to get a word in edgewise, Sally commented, "With God, all things are possible. He will make a way where there is no way."

"Amen!" was Randy's response.

Chapter 3

Randy slept like a baby once he was settled into his old room at Sally's. He was thankful that she had painted the room a cheerful color. After the drab surroundings in prison, he drank in the vibrancy of those walls.

For several years, Sally kept hoping Randy would be home any day, leaving his room exactly the way he left it. Eventually, she put away the posters from the walls, and boxed up his trophies and awards.

Even when he came to visit, he rarely spent the night. Nothing else changed until he was ready to come home. With his release from prison, she had a reason at last to paint the walls, and get new linens for the bed and bathroom.

Since he had earned such a large amount of money from his previous 'employment,' as well as his own actions, he had been able to get himself some really nice furniture and electronics. Now everything was in place. His clothes were hung in the closet, and his few books were on the shelf.

She told him that he was welcome to stay here as long as he needed.

He thanked her for the offer but assured her that once he was established in a paying position, he would want to be out on his own, renting his own place.

She understood, but hoped that it wouldn't be right away. She was going to enjoy having him around!

When he was arrested, he gladly gave the cash that he had accumulated from these activities back to the people from whom he had taken anything.

Randy had not wanted to hang onto anything that didn't belong to him. His salvation had changed his heart in such a way that now neither things nor money was any longer his god.

No amount of wealth compared to the peace he experienced when he prayed that Sunday at church. Something as simple as a prayer had changed his life forever! He was still amazed that God loved him in spite of the life he had lived.

He had been forgiven, the slate wiped clean, and he truly was a new man. Learning all he could about this new life while he was incarcerated only reinforced his decision. Never would he go back to that other life. It now held no appeal at all. He saw men of many ages in jail for the third and fourth time. They mostly appeared beaten down or were bullies and amassed the same sort of friends. This convinced him that he would never become one of those men. His life was too important to repeat his mistakes. He knew that God had reached out to him and saved him from becoming a lifetime criminal. His new life would be Amazing!

★ ★ ★

The next day, Sally was busy making lunch when Randy appeared in the doorway to the kitchen. She had taken a few days off work so that she could welcome her son and help him get settled.

"It's about time, Sleepyhead!" she laughed.

Yawning, Randy rubbed his stomach as he grinned at his mom. "I must have been tired. I haven't slept that long since I was a teenager!"

"It's probably because you are now a free man. You no longer have to worry about anything," she responded.

"That's for sure. It feels so good to not have a guard watching my every move, or making snide remarks about my faith or reading my Bible."

"I'm so thankful that you're letting me stay here, Mom. How you ever put up with me for all these years is beyond me," he said as he reached for the cup of coffee that Sally handed him.

"You and I both know that it was the Lord who kept us through those long years. You were never out of His sight or my prayers," Sally replied

She placed a ham sandwich on a plate. Handing it to Randy, she also put a bowl of chips next to him. He sat down at the table in the same chair he always used when he was a kid.

After offering a prayer of thanks for the food, Randy dove into the simple meal. While he was eating, he thought about his life.

Leaving home at seventeen after his dad died unexpectedly was not the wisest thing he'd ever done. Without a high school diploma, he found it hard to find a job. Eventually, he got his equivalency certificate. That helped some.

The things he had to do to survive were things he'd rather not think about. Thankfully, now they were covered by the blood of Jesus. He would no longer be responsible for them. He'd been forgiven of all! Sadly, he did have to pay a price with consequences that kept him locked up for longer than he liked. Now those times were over. He was making a fresh start.

While struggling to make it on his own, it had taken several years before he even felt ready to make contact again with his mom. By the time he was twenty-six, nearly ten years after he left, he had called her out of the blue.

After that, they met for dinner or lunch every few weeks. He kept his true activities to himself. No need to burden Sally with the truth. She seemed delighted to have him back in her life.

Before he came to faith, he was amazed that she could forgive him and welcome him so readily into her life again. Being with her usually made him feel guilty—even though she never said a thing. Her acceptance left him confused but glad at the same time. It was after he was on the same page with her spiritually that he finally understood.

Now, he was a grown man of thirty-four. It was time he started paying back his mom for all her sacrifices for him. He could never recoup those lost years, but maybe he could bring her some happiness for the ones to come. He certainly hoped that would be true.

First thing, he needed to get his driver's license renewed. Then he had to set up the community service hours he was required to fulfill. His first meeting with his parole officer would define what was expected of him and for how long.

Then, he needed to get a job. After getting the other things out of the way, he would call the bakery owner that had been recommended to him. Hopefully, the guy would be willing to take him on. Otherwise, he wasn't sure what he'd do.

Instead of letting anxiety overwhelm him about his future, he chose to put it all in God's hands. Where better could it be?

Whenever he would start to get anxious about succeeding, he would again turn to the Lord for assurance that he was on the right track. With that assurance, he knew he was no longer alone. He had a Helper with him every step of the way.

★ ★ ★

Sally took him to DMV, and shortly he walked out with his renewed license and a thankful heart.

That afternoon, he met with Officer Peters and they went over the requirements he was expected to fulfill in the next year. If he met with the man's approval, he could move forward to calling about the job.

Soon, he was picking up trash around the main town center every afternoon for an hour a day, six days a week. That would last for at least six months to a year, depending on Officer Peters and his watchful eye.

★ ★ ★

Following a simple but tasty lunch fixed by Sally a few days later, Randy felt he was ready to make an appointment with Mr. Foster.

He made the call, and after showering and dressing in his best slacks and dress shirt, Randy asked Sally if he could use her car for his interview. Sally willingly handed him her keys with a hug and a prayer for favor.

Randy drove to the neighborhood bakery where he hoped to find employment. Parking on the side street around the corner from the establishment, he squared his shoulders, took a deep breath, and entered the aroma-packed store.

His creative juices were aroused when he observed the various baked goods in the glass-enclosed cases, as well as the lovely wedding cake on display. Or was it because of the scent? Either way, he hoped and prayed that the person he was seeing would be willing to give him a chance.

The place was busy with several customers picking out a dozen of this, a half dozen of that. Someone was at a desk taking an order for a special cake.

Taking in his surroundings, Randy liked the bright, attractive atmosphere of the store. Would he fit in? Would he be able to create those extravagant cakes? With the right training, he felt that he could prove himself worth the hire.

When the older man behind the counter finished with all the other customers, there was a lull in business. He turned to Randy and asked what he'd like.

Randy said, "I'm Randy Burnett. Are you Mr. Foster? I have an appointment at three."

"Ah, yes. You're right on time. I like that. I'm Fred Foster. Let's go into my office," he said as he led Randy behind the counter into his clean but messy space.

Clearing some files off of the chair in front of his desk, he said, "So, tell me about yourself, Randy. You don't mind if I call you Randy? You can call me Fred," he offered.

When Randy nodded his approval, Fred smiled and sat down at his crowded desk.

"Well, sir, Fred, as you know I was just released from prison. I'm not proud of what I did to get there. But that life is behind me. I became a Christian—the day I was arrested, actually. Since then, I've been growing in my faith. The lure of wealth and things no longer appeals to me. Now, I just want to work at something I love. Getting paid will be the icing on the cake, so to speak!" Randy laughed.

"Do you mind telling me what you did to land yourself in prison?" asked the kindly older gentleman.

"Not at all. As I said, I'm not proud of my behavior. I was raised better than that." Randy went on to tell Fred of his leaving home before he could graduate. He left out some of the more disgusting things he did to stay alive.

He told him about the too-good-to-be-true offer from the *Boss*. He also admitted to his own schemes that netted him a fair amount of cash.

"As you may have read in the papers a little over eight years ago, my *Boss* was arrested. I was his patsy."

Fred smiled his approval as he said, "Yes, I did read about that,"

Adjusting his glasses, Fred continued, "I, too, am a Christian. I like to help young people like you to get on their feet after they have paid for their mistakes. I can see that you are truly sorry for what you did, making amends where possible. I think we can work something out," he added.

Randy relaxed for the first time since he sat down.

"Why do you want to learn to be a baker?"

"The only occupation that was available to me while I was locked up was working with the cook. I found that creating something from nothing gave me great satisfaction. Although I like cooking generally, creating a baked concoction just seemed to grab my attention. Can't really explain it any better than that," Randy admitted.

"Might it have something to do with God leading you?"

"Yes, sir, I think you are right. I would never have known that I could do anything like that if I hadn't been given the job in the first place.

"The prison cook had been a pastry expert before he got in trouble with the law. Maybe it was his passion that rubbed off on me. Anyway, if you'll give me a chance, I'll try not to disappoint you," Randy finished.

Mr. Foster reached his hand across the desk to Randy shaking his hand with vigor. "I think we will be a good fit. You can start tomorrow at 4:30—in the morning. We have to get a head start on the day with fresh breads, scones, etc."

Randy gulped silently at the early hour but nodded.

"I'll be giving you hands-on training. I've found that works much better than me talking and you taking notes. Whatever you attempt to make that doesn't quite cut the mustard, makes for a great breakfast!" Fred said, laughing.

"Thank you, Mr. Foster, ur, Fred. I'll do my best to not let you down. You don't know how much this means to me," Randy said, shaking the man's hand.

"Oh, I think I can imagine. You see, I was once in your position. If it hadn't been for an older man who took a chance on me, I wouldn't be here today, doing what I love," confessed the kind man with a smile on his face.

Astonished, Randy smiled back, thankful that he didn't have to try to make this gentleman understand. Only God could have sent him to just the right place.

They took care of paperwork in short order, and soon Randy was rising from his seat.

"I'll be here bright and early in the morning. And thank you, again, for taking a chance on me. I will try to meet your expectations."

"Don't think I'll make it easy on you! You'll have to pull your weight around here. But if you prove to be as good at this job as we both hope, I'm not worried," replied his new employer.

Shaking hands again, the two men walked back into the sweet-smelling front of the store. Mr. Foster introduced him to Larry, another employee in the shop. Fred told him there were a couple of young women who were on the payroll but were only there on week-ends or during the summer. He'd meet them later.

Leaving the bakery, Randy marveled at the goodness of His Savior for leading him to just the right place. To learn quickly, he would depend on Him to help him, and to be a star employee.

Heading back to Sally's home, his head was filled with ideas for baked goods the likes of which no one had yet seen.

Maybe he was getting ahead of himself! He really wanted to be able to create appealing food that people would be waiting in line to buy. The satisfaction of doing something to please others rather than himself was almost pay enough. Almost!

Chapter 4

Joan Travis was sitting in her comfortable recliner on a pleasant Sunday afternoon. Her thoughts turned to the many events in her life that had shaped her into the woman she was today. She began to talk to the Lord about some of them, "After our daughter Julie died, and Gary bailed out of our marriage, I'm so thankful that I returned to my left-behind faith. In reestablishing my relationship with You, Lord, I found the peace and contentment that had been lacking in my previously hectic life."

Thoughts of her nursing career, eventually becoming head of nursing at the hospital, brought thankfulness to her heart. Being able to pass more and more responsibility to others while continuing in her position brought her the respect and admiration of the entire hospital staff. She knew that when given the chance, most people could work out their problems and differences if only someone would take the time to listen.

Continuing her conversation with her Savior, Joan said, "Thank You for helping me to be quiet in the midst of turmoil. It has become my most powerful advantage when it comes to my walk of faith. It humbles me that You have given me a tender heart, and a listening ear. Many people have come to me for advice and prayer. The results of those hundreds of prayers make it seem as though I know how to get things done! Hardly! If it weren't for Your intervention and compassion, nothing would have changed for anyone."

Thinking of her many prayer journals reminded her again of the faithfulness of God, though not every prayer was answered in the way she or others thought they wanted. And some things were still waiting in the balance for divine intervention. However, many, many other petitions had been answered above and beyond anything she or they could have hoped for or imagined.

"Lord, You know how I love to learn all I can about You, and to teach as many as I can the things I am learning, no matter if they have been easy or hard. Your telling me to be open, transparent, and vulnerable has proven to be a blessing, not something to avoid. I want to always be approachable, trustworthy, and a valued friend.

"Those who enjoy my Sunday school lessons each week comment on my insight and understanding. We both know that it comes from You. The classes are fun, exciting, and enriching. Many of those women have become my dearest friends."

Going on down her list of those things for which she is grateful, Joan continues her conversation with her Best Friend, "My son Philip and his wife Penny have given me my adorable grandson, Lyle. He brings so much joy to all of us. How can I ever thank You for all that you have done and continue to do for me, my family, and my friends?"

Just then, there was a knock at her door. She wasn't expecting company. Maybe it was a delivery man, but she couldn't remember ordering anything recently. As she made her way to the door, she ran her fingers through her hair, checking her make-up in the hall mirror. No sense in frightening the person away!

Peering through the peephole made her stop in her tracks. No! It couldn't be!

Slowly opening the door, she stared into the older, but still-handsome, face of her long-departed ex-husband.

"Hello, Joan, I guess you're surprised to see me," he said.

So stunned that she was speechless, Joan just nodded her head. It had been more than twenty years since she had seen or heard from Gary. He not only bailed out of the marriage, but he also abandoned their son, Philip. No contact, no birthday or Christmas cards, nothing but the monthly child-support checks until Philip reached eighteen.

Her stomach was doing flip-flops, and her heart had started beating so fast she felt faint. Trying to gather her wits about her, Joan asked, "What do you want?"

"Is that any way to greet your first love?" he asked with a tight smile on his face that wasn't reflected in his eyes.

Sighing, Joan motioned for him to come in as she headed to the living room. Once they were seated, she asked again, "What do you want."

"I came to see how you are. This is a nice place. Looks like you're doing okay for yourself."

"God is blessing me. I have no complaints," she responded. *Except for seeing you out of the blue,* she wanted to say.

"Knowing you, you've worked yourself pretty hard to make something of yourself. You always were a go-getter."

"Why don't you just tell me why you're here, Gary?"

"Okay, I'll cut to the chase. I want to see Philip. I've heard that he's married and has a kid. I'd like to see my grandchild, too."

"Why now, after all these years? You dropped out of his life without so much as a backward glance. He was heart-broken for months when you didn't call or make any contact with him. He was sure for a long time that he'd done something to make you leave us."

"That's crazy. He wasn't to blame for my taking off," Gary angrily replied.

"To a child, that's what it seemed. You not only abandoned me, you abandoned him. It took a long time for him to finally get used to the idea that you weren't coming back," Joan replied softly.

"Yeah, I suppose he could have thought that. I just figured he'd be better off without me."

"Why? Every boy wants his father to love and notice him. He was devastated."

"Okay, okay, enough with the guilt trip. Are you going to let me know how to get in touch with him or not?" Gary's anger was surfacing again.

Joan thought, *what has made him so angry? He used to be so easygoing, kind, and thoughtful.*

With a quick prayer for guidance, Joan replied, "No, I don't think that would be a good idea."

Rising from his chair, Gary loomed over her, "Why not? He's my son, too, you know. I have a right to know where he is."

"You gave up that right when you left us," Joan answered without losing her temper.

"You are a piece of work, you know that? Always trying to control everyone else's life. No wonder you drove me away. I guess I'll just have to find out the information another way. I thought you'd be happy that I want to be a grandfather to my grandchild," he said as he stormed out, slamming the door.

Joan sat in stunned silence. What had just happened? *Lord, help me,* she prayed. Did I do the wrong thing? She didn't think so. Her mother's heart ached for all the years of Philip's waiting and hoping for his dad to return. It was only after she led her son to the Lord that he was able to forgive his dad and move on in his life.

She thought that she had done the same. Now, she wasn't so sure. Old feelings that had been buried began to surface. Hadn't she forgiven Gary? Then why did she now want to throttle him? How could he be so selfish? What had she seen in him in the first place? Sure, he was handsome, self-assured, capable, but the pressure of their daughter Julie's needs and her own involvement in getting those met had driven him to run.

When Joan had reestablished her relationship with the Lord, the first thing she did was forgive Gary. But the old hurts were still there after all.

She surmised it was true that you can forgive someone, but you don't have to love them or what they did to hurt you. Now what was she supposed to do?

Chapter 5

Randy walked into the kitchen where Sally was preparing dinner. "Anything I can do to help?" he asked.

"No thanks, honey, you work hard, I don't mind fixing this for you," she replied.

"I know, Mom, but I'm not a little boy anymore!" he said, laughing.

"Okay, why don't you get the beans ready?" she said, relenting. Showing him what to do, she added, "It's just that I'm so happy to have you around, that anytime I can fix meals for you it is my pleasure."

"I understand, Mom, but I need to learn more about cooking than baking or I'll starve. Why don't we share the meal preparations all the time? What better way for me to learn than you showing me all your tricks of the trade?" He smiled as he sat down at the kitchen table with a pile of green beans and began snapping them into a pan.

"That's a great idea," Sally answered. "I'd love to teach you all I know, which isn't as much as you might think. Tonight is a good start. We could work together on the weekly menu and see if we can give you a good boost in the culinary arts department outside of baking. Maybe you can teach me some of your baking tricks too."

"That sounds like a doable plan, Mom."

"Besides all that," he added. "I'm going to have to think about getting my own place pretty soon. Don't get me wrong, I love being here with you. But…"

"I know," she answered. "You're all grown up and you don't want to let your 'mommy' take care of you!"

Smiling, he got up and hugged her tightly from behind. "That's what I love about you. You know me so well. I love having my 'mommy' take care of me, but that can get to be a habit that isn't good for my future. What if I want to get married some day? I'd want to help my wife in the kitchen, but would have to call you to know what to do!!"

Sally held her sides laughing. "You wouldn't do that! Would you?"

"You never can tell! I've heard of many women that call their moms about that special recipe, after they are married," he said with a wide grin.

"Are you speaking of anyone in particular? Or is it a generic 'someday' comment?"

Laughing, Randy said, "No one in particular as yet, so rest easy. I'll let you know if anyone comes along that makes me want to even think about getting married."

"Fair enough," chuckled Sally.

"Let's table this discussion for now. What else can I do for you?" he asked as he poured water into the pan of beans and set them on the burner.

They finished fixing the meal together, enjoying each other's company. Sally mused about her grown-up son. Who would have thought that this day would come? Her prayers had been answered in ways that even she could not have anticipated.

Randy's job at the bakery had him out the door before the rooster crowed, but it also allowed him to be home before dark. Many days, he took a nap before Sally got home so that he would not yawn in her face during dinner.

They had settled into a comfortable routine, but both of them knew instinctively that it was to be short-lived.

She was reminded about the well-known passage in the book of Genesis where Joseph speaks of the evil that was intended for him, yet God turned it to good, to bring prosperity to many people. The evil that dragged her son into so many dark places over the years was turned into a good thing that had brought him a prosperous job and, hopefully, a joyful lifetime some day with a wonderful woman of God.

While they ate, Sally asked, "Have you tried finding a place of your own? Or will you start soon?"

Randy swallowed a mouthful of the beef stroganoff before answering her.

"I can't really afford much on my salary, especially since I'm now making car payments every month. Actually, I have been checking out a few places. A couple of studio apartments looked promising. Nothing definite yet, so don't worry."

"Don't you know that worry is what mom's do best?" Sally laughed. Then she added, "But with God, there don't have to be any worries. He's got us covered all the time."

"So right you are," Randy agreed.

★ ★ ★

A few weeks later at the bakery, Randy was finishing with a special order when Fred asked to see him as soon as he was done. Hoping that he wasn't going to be fired, Randy placed the tray of pastries into the cooler and headed to his boss's office.

"Sit down, Randy. And take that worried expression off your face," Fred instructed with a smile.

Letting out his breath, Randy seated himself in the small chair.

"First of all, I want to commend you for how fast you are learning to make the delicacies we sell. I'm impressed, to say the least. You are a quick study, like a sponge absorbing whatever I show you."

Randy didn't know what to say other than, "Thank you, Fred. Giving me this chance was truly an answer to prayer. You'll never know how much I appreciate your patience with me."

"I think it's time for you to up your knowledge."

"What do you mean?"

Fred pulled a brochure from his desk drawer and handed it to Randy.

The young man took it and began reading the information about advanced baking classes that were going to be taught at the local college, as well as a couple of entrepreneurial courses for new business owners.

With a question in his eyes, he scrutinized Fred.

"I think you should learn everything you can about this business, especially all of the things that I can't teach you. I'd be happy to pay your tuition if you promise to keep working for me when you're done."

Randy sat dumbfounded. "You'd do that for me? Why?"

"Because I see so much potential in you. Who knows? The sky is the limit. What do you say?" he asked with hope in his expression.

"Wow, Fred. This would be an incredible experience. Are you sure you trust me that much? I mean, I haven't been here that long. Why would you do this for me?"

"Let's just say that you're the son I never had. I want to invest in your future. Not only will it benefit you, but in the meantime, I'd get some of the benefit as well. As I've said, I'm not getting any younger. I would like to see you take over here, maybe opening other shops in the area."

Randy could hardly believe what he was hearing. The classes began in a few weeks, lasting for three semesters, around eighteen months. With a bit of juggling, he could help Fred in the mornings, take classes in the afternoons, do his hour of community service, and sleep whenever he could fit it in!

"Can I let you know in a few days? I need to process this and pray about it."

"Okay, but you need to get registered as soon as possible to be sure that the classes aren't filled. How about giving me your decision day after tomorrow? That will give you time to get your schedule set up, buy your books, and prepare yourself for this new adventure."

"I'd still come in every morning to help you, though. I don't want to let you carry the load by yourself."

Fred reached his hand across the desk. "Deal. But classes will come before work. Got it? I know you can do this."

Randy shook his employer's hand and walked out of the office in a daze. *'Boy, God, when You want to give a guy some direction, You sure do it from out of the blue. I never saw this coming. Show me Your plan and help me walk it out,* he prayed as he headed to the prep area.

CHAPTER 6

Settling into his new position in the bakery, Randy enjoyed the creative process as well as interacting with the customers. His employer, Fred, set aside each morning before opening hours to train his new apprentice.

Being on his feet for hours at a time was almost as tiring as trying to remember everything his mentor was teaching him.

After a full morning at the bakery, two classes a week at school, he also had to add at least an hour of his community service. Many afternoons, he went home and straight to bed for a nap before dinner. Sally understood the pressure of a new job and school, so she didn't push him to be sociable after a long day.

When he did feel like interacting, they had some revealing conversations.

One evening, Randy answered his mom's questions about his new work.

"Not measuring and mixing ingredients properly has resulted in lots of mishaps. I've learned my lessons the hard way, like leaving something in the oven too long, or over stirring which resulted in tough dough.

"Fred is a hard-hitting but careful teacher. He doesn't want me to become discouraged with my failures. Instead, he praises my successes, and instructs through the mistakes."

Sally interjected, "Isn't that just like life?"

"You're so right. Once I got the basics under my belt, Fred moved on to the more intricate delicacies. Decorative pie crust, frosted cupcakes, and batter-dipped ice cream became the newest instruction instruments.

"I never knew that there were so many different kinds of baked goods. All I ever saw you do was use a box mix to make cookies or cakes. Working every day, you probably didn't have time to put together anything more complicated than the basics; and you always bought pies and specially-decorated cakes at a bakery just like Fred's."

"So true. As much as I wanted to do those things, after working all day, adding one more thing to my plate just wasn't appealing. Besides, no one ever complained!"

"Not me, that's for sure. You don't miss what you've never had!"

At this, Sally threw the couch pillow at him, laughing.

Ducking out of the way, Randy pitched it back at her. It was so satisfying to be able to enjoy one another like this. Life is good; God is good.

"Well, now I am the one behind the counter, creating these delightful buttery crisp scones and tarts, as well as all the other varieties that are available beneath the glass. It's enough to give anyone a sugar headache! But I love it!"

"I'm so glad you've found your niche. Who would have thought?" Sally replied.

"Yeah, the more I learn, the more I want to learn. And in my classes I've learned that just the different kinds of breads are enough to keep me busy for weeks, applying the right techniques. Beyond that are the biscuits, rolls, muffins, and bars. Not to mention the petit fours and macaroons. The list goes on and on. I will need years to perfect every one of the recipes that Fred guards so carefully.

"At this point, I'm not sure if I want to pursue a full college degree to become a pastry chef, or just be satisfied mining Fred's vast knowledge. Maybe, one day, I could own and operate my own bakery."

Sally added, "There's a favorite Scripture of mine that says the Lord grants us the desires of our hearts."

Randy said, "Yes, I know that one. The beginning of the verse is just as important. We are to delight ourselves in the Lord, and *then* He gives us those dreams and desires."

"Absolutely!"

"Being a master baker means more responsibility than I'm willing to take on, at least anytime in the near future. Fred's tutelage and my classes will keep me busy enough for now.

"There is so much to learn. You don't just throw the ingredients into a bowl and mix! Measuring and timing are crucial to a successful outcome.

"I hate to admit it but one day, a whole batch of lemon bars had to be thrown away when I used too much of one thing and not enough of something else. It wasn't until I bit into a broken, unsellable bar, that I knew I'd done something wrong.

"The best part is that Fred didn't begrudge the waste. He said that what I do create and sell more than makes up for the few errors I encounter."

"What a remarkable man he is. Truly, the Lord has done quite a work in his life," Sally offered.

"He told me that the mistakes would be lessened as I got better at what I was doing because that was how he learned as well. Being in a hurry to finish mixing a batter always leads to disaster. Learning to slow down and carefully taking each step one at a time has become my mantra for each day."

"That's all that's expected of any of us," Sally agreed. "When I first went to work for that lawyer, I didn't know anything. But with careful teaching, I learned quickly. When he died, I could take that knowledge into my current position. Everything worthwhile takes time."

"So right. When I am rewarded with a perfect scone or muffin, I can't help beaming with pride. Then I remind myself that without the Lord's strength, I'd never be able to have the patience necessary to see the completion of my tasks.

"The more I lean on the Savior, the fewer mistakes I make. That still, small voice has helped me to avoid disaster on more than one occasion. I also realized I don't know everything just because I successfully accomplish one or two recipes. Maturing in my faith is helping me to mature in my approach to this new venture."

★ ★ ★

The next day while decorating a cake, Randy's thoughts took him back to the past, when he was so obsessed with getting money and things, that he hadn't thought further than the next theft.

There had been no incentive to learn a real trade or find a promotion-promising job. At first, his menial jobs gave him enough income to rent a dingy apartment. The meager salaries had filled his stomach with fast food and provided second-hand clothes.

But the money he made working for the *Boss,* and for himself, had netted him quite a great deal of cash.

He never anticipated beyond the moment, living for the now, without any thought for the future.

The problem was, the more he had, the more he wanted. He was never satisfied. That new car made him feel like he was king of the road. But he had to drive his old clunker to accomplish his *side* jobs.

It was almost as if he was a split-personality. One life was day-to-day grind. The other was risk-filled and exciting. But he couldn't live completely in either one.

How had he been so dumb? Immaturity had played a great part in his thinking. Also, society pushed you to *have it all* without telling you how to achieve this pinnacle of success. The idea of having everything you wanted, now, before you earned it, was such a selfish and childish way to live.

He was learning that it took just plain hard work to feel good about himself and what he accomplished in a day. He wished he could tell some of those guys he met in prison what he was experiencing. Working hard for a goal, achieving it, and then setting higher goals for yourself were what gave a person his self-esteem. Not stepping all over others to get to the top.

Taking what you wanted without having to suffer the consequences hadn't worked either. He had eight years behind bars to show for it.

The buzzer on the huge oven at the back of the kitchen brought Randy out of his reverie. Pulling a large tray of biscuits from the hot enclosure, he set the tray down on the stainless steel worktop.

These would be delicious! Another sense of achievement covered Randy's face with a smile. What a life! He was having his cake and eating it too! What more could he want?

★ ★ ★

The next day, Randy met with his parole officer to update him on his progress. These weekly meetings were another way in which he had to measure up to the new standards of his life.

"How's it going Burnett?" asked Officer Peters, in a none-too-friendly manner.

Knowing that he was on a short leash with the man, Randy tried to be as honest as possible. He didn't want to slip up or give the guy a reason to question his ability to function on the outside.

"It's going pretty well. As you know, I've been working for Mr. Foster now for several months. I couldn't ask for a better opportunity than to learn from him. And my classes at the community college are going well. I'm so thankful for these chances to prove myself."

"Okay, okay, I get it. What else is going on? Anything I should know about? Any other 'opportunities' come your way?" asked the skeptical officer.

Randy knew exactly what he had in mind. "No, sir! I'm keeping my 'nose clean' this time around. No more of those questionable activities for me."

"Glad to hear it. I must say, you've made quite a turnaround for someone who got himself into so much hot water not that long ago. You sure you don't want to find another 'Boss' to help you get ahead, to pad your pockets?" the rather intimidating representative of the law sneered.

Knowing that the man didn't believe him when Randy tried to tell him of his conversion to Christ, that He made all the difference, Randy just sat up a bit straighter and replied, "I'm perfectly content with where I am at this point in my life. All the other trappings that I once had to have are not important to me anymore."

"Yeah, right, so you say. I'm still keeping my eye on you, Burnett. No one changes that much just 'cause they were behind bars, or had some religious 'conversion,' as you say. They usually come out doing worse things than they did before they were caught in the first place," Officer Peters replied.

Randy had been praying for an opportunity to explain more about his relationship with Christ, but the man was a closed book. The younger man would just have to prove himself by his actions and attitude. He didn't let the disbelieving officer dissuade him from his course. Even the times Officer Peters had made surprise visits to the bakery had not upset him. The man was just doing his job. Thus far, he had nothing about Randy's new life with which to find objection.

"Still living with your mama?"

"Yes, until I can afford to find my own place, and I'm making payments on a second-hand car so I don't have to use hers all the time. She was willing to take the bus to work, but I didn't like putting her out. But there aren't any busses running when I need to be at work in the mornings, so there was no other option right now."

The Officer begrudgingly replied, "Well, that's a good thing. Hope you make it."

Officer Peters rose from his chair in the coffee shop where they met after Randy got off work every Friday, "Same time next week." And with that, he was out the door.

Randy watched the man walk away shaking his head. The jaded parole officer just didn't know what to make of a convicted criminal making such a one-eighty in his life. Only time would prove the truth of what had taken place to make Randy a new man, inside and out.

CHAPTER 7

A few months later, Randy was just putting a tray of blueberry muffins into the bakery case when the bell above the door jingled. Glancing up after closing the glass partition in the back of the case, he saw a lovely young woman entering the shop.

"May I help you?" he asked in his best salesman's voice.

Smiling shyly, she said, "I hope so. I want to get just the right pastries for a meeting in a couple of weeks."

Standing up a little straighter, Randy said, "May I ask what kind of gathering? Sometimes the people who will be there dictate the types of delicacies they would enjoy."

Smiling back at the handsome, thirty-something young man, Gerry Smart thought about his assessment.

Blushing slightly, she answered, "Yes. That makes sense. I'm a fourth-grade teacher at Parker Elementary. Several of us are making a presentation at a social gathering of school board members for some before-and-after-school programs that my co-teachers and I developed for underprivileged kids."

"Okay, how many people, and why would you be feeding them?" he questioned.

Gerry grinned back at his question, "As to the number of people who will attend, I believe there are twenty members of the board, as well as the other presenters who will be there, about thirty all together. We thought that an informal meeting would help put everyone at ease; and make it possible for us to present our ideas without feeling like we were on trial at a formal board meeting. All of the teachers at the school have banded together to try to help our community produce successful school graduates.

"Right now, many of the kids never make it that far. I come from a middle-class family who did not have to struggle much with life's needs. But the school where I teach is in a poorer section of the city. Every day I see kids with barely enough to wear or eat, who just seem to need someone to care for them."

He could feel her empathy as she spoke. He felt a definite connection to her.

"Let me get some more information from you," he said. "When and where will this event take place?"

In his best detective voice he said, "Just the facts, ma'am!"

Laughing, she told him that the meeting would take place the following Friday evening at the neighborhood community center near her school. "We're not really trying to bribe the board members, but we also don't want them to forget about us and our requests."

"I'm sure they won't forget you," he agreed. This brought a huge smile to her face.

He went on, "Once we finish with this order, do you have time to share your ideas with me? Maybe I can also be of help. I'm just learning that the creative side of my personality is a gift from God. I'm sure you would agree that He can use anyone to show His limitless possibilities," he said, hoping she would not be offended by his remark.

Relaxing for the first time since she entered the establishment, Gerry grinned at the handsome young man.

"I couldn't agree with you more. I thank God every day for every idea He gives me. I may be good, but He's even better!"

Laughing together, they again turned to the matter at hand. Once Gerry had made her selections and placed her order for the various pastries and desserts to offer her guests, she told Randy that she would be right back.

He watched her exit the shop, hoping that she wasn't giving him the brush off. There was something intriguing about her that made him want to get to know her better.

Soon, Gerry was back with a large folder in her arm.

Since the bakery was not busy, Randy led her to one of the three small café tables near the window. The bakery also sold a limited number of flavored coffees and teas along with their baked creations. This encouraged the customers to take a few minutes to enjoy their purchases along with quiet conversation.

"By the way, my name is Randy Burnett," he said as he extended his hand to her. Taking it with a gentle shake, she replied, "Gerry Smart."

"Nice to meet you," they said in unison, laughing.

Randy asked if she'd like something to drink, but Gerry declined. Randy assumed that she didn't want to spend the extra cash right now since she had just placed such a large order. Ignoring her comment, he went behind the counter and poured two cups of herbal tea. Bringing them to the table, he said, "On the house."

Her grateful smile told him he had guessed correctly.

She opened the folder carefully, like a mother with her precious child. Randy could relate to her on so many levels.

Showing him each proposal, one at a time, she explained the types of programs, why she had chosen them, and how she had come up with the ideas in the first place.

Realizing that she was caught up in the moment, Gerry stopped and took a small sip of her tea.

"I guess you could say that I'm just a bit enthusiastic!" she admitted.

Randy continued to peruse through the several pages of ideas before commenting.

"These are great! You are very talented! Of course, I'm no expert, but I can certainly see kids enjoying these programs and activities."

His comments brought another huge smile to her face. "Thank you," she said quietly. "It means a lot to me to get good feedback from someone who isn't connected to the school."

"Like I said, I'm no authority. I know that you will go far. I truly wish you well. You'll have to let me know how your meeting turns out. Is this the first one you've had?" he asked.

"No, we've tried before to get some of these programs and ideas implemented, but been turned down. There are several new members to the board who, individually, like our ideas."

Continuing, she said, "My co-teachers and I have worked hard to make our ideas seem doable. A couple of times we were told that we were naïve in our outlook, and not to come back unless we had something substantial to offer."

"That must have been a little daunting," he said.

"No doubt about it. I was shaking in my boots for a while until I realized that I wasn't alone in this venture. If God is behind it, and I think He is, then it would succeed."

"Absolutely," agreed Randy.

Changing the subject, he asked her where she went to church.

"I've been going to Bellwood Community Church ever since college."

She went on to tell him about her family. Hearing the gospel message for the first time when she was in college, she immediately accepted the Lord as her Savior. Instead of feeling like she was on the outside observing those on the inside, she now felt like she really belonged.

Amazement filled Randy as he listened to her talk about her life, her experiences, and her faith. He was grateful that no customers came along to interrupt his afternoon with this fascinating young woman.

Gerry continued, "My Sunday school teacher, Joan Travis, has helped me so much to grow in my faith. She is so grounded in the Word. She always makes us think about what we are learning. As she said, we don't need to just learn facts. We need to know how to apply what we're learning to our daily lives."

Again, Randy sat in amazement. Joan had been such a great influence on his mom, Sally. What a small world!

When she finally realized that she had been talking about herself for quite a while, Gerry apologized for monopolizing the conversation.

"That's fine," Randy replied. "No need to apologize. I've enjoyed hearing about your journey."

Feeling that she would understand, he went on to tell her about himself. His life of crime, his salvation, his imprisonment, and now his passion for baking were all included in the short monologue.

He concluded with, "Joan Travis has been praying for me for years. She led my mom, Sally, to the Lord a long time ago. They've become great friends. If it hadn't been for her encouragement along the way, I don't know if my mom would have been able to make it through the years when I was out of touch. I regret that decision more than I can say. I'm so grateful for people I don't even know who have prayed for me. I'm here now, redeemed, washed clean, and starting over," he finished.

"I remember her asking us to pray for you! Wow! We serve a great big God, don't we?"

"You can say that again," Randy agreed.

"We serve a great big God!" she said laughing.

Joining with her, Randy decided that this had been a most momentous day. He hoped that it might be the beginning of something even more exciting.

CHAPTER 8

After she picked up her order a week later, Randy agonized for days over whether or not he should call Gerry and ask her for a date. What if she had just been nice when she heard his story? What if she really thought he had been too corrupt for her to be associated with him? What if his past completely turned her off? What if she wasn't even the slightest bit attracted to him? What if his profession of faith didn't convince her that he had changed? What if she said, "Yes?"

Marshalling all his nerve, he picked up his phone and punched in her number before he could change his mind. He had asked for guidance in this new friendship and possible relationship. Since there had been no red light, he hoped he was doing the right thing, and that she would be agreeable to seeing him again.

Their brief conversation that day in the bakery had shown him that she was someone he wanted to get to know better. When she came back the second time to pick up her large order, he tried to remember to be himself, and not try to charm her into liking him.

"Hello," Gerry said when she answered the phone.

"Hi, Gerry, this is Randy Burnett—from the bakery," he said tentatively.

"Oh, hi, Randy, it's nice to hear from you. How have you been?" It was only last week when they had last talked at the store, but—so far, so good.

"I was wondering if you'd like to go to a program that my church is having this Friday evening. It's being put on by the youth department to showcase the talents of many of the kids," he said, trying not to rush his words.

"That's sounds lovely. Seeing young adults using their gifts to glorify God always blesses me. What time?"

Breathing a sigh of relief, Randy answered, "It's at seven-thirty. We could go get something to eat first if you'd like."

"Oh, food, and fun! I like that!" she responded.

"Great. Let me have your address. Is five o'clock okay for dinner? We can go to that new Italian restaurant that just opened not far from the church," he offered.

"Can we make it five-fifteen? I don't usually get home from school until nearly five and will need a few minutes to freshen up," Gerry asked.

"Of course. We could go to the diner instead if you like. Their service is faster." *We can save the Italian place for another date if this works out,* he thought.

"Sounds like a plan." She rattled off her address for him. "I'm so glad you called."

Once they hung up, Randy let out a huge breath. *Whew, that was a rush!* He had not dated much over the course of his life. He'd been too busy trying to make money and buy things to fill that void inside. When he came to the Lord, the hole was no longer empty. Now, he enjoyed life without the extras, not even missing all the doodads he thought would give him satisfaction.

Informing his mom about his date, she said, "You have to tell me more about this young lady. You said that you met her at work. What else do you know about her?"

Randy hadn't said much to Sally about the one who was occupying his mind most of the time. He took a breath and then said, "Her name is Gerry Smart. She goes to the same church as your friend, Joan, and is in her Sunday school class. She's an elementary school teacher, and she's a committed believer. She's beautiful and she just radiates the love of Jesus!"

Sally just giggled before replying, "Good for you in recognizing what's most important—what's on the inside. I'll be praying for you, son. I know that if God has brought her to you, she's perfect!"

"I'm praying that's so. I don't want to get ahead of Him," replied Randy.

Later that evening while lying in bed, sleep eluded him. Thinking back to his days behind bars, Randy could not help but thank God for those times when He intervened in what could have been some serious, life-changing exchanges with other prisoners.

It was like a movie running behind his closed eyes as Randy saw again the hand of God on his life.

The roughest of the prisoners, Gido, seemed to be able to get anyone to do anything he commanded. He had decided that Randy needed to be 'taught a lesson' in manners when Randy didn't address him as "Sir" whenever he had opportunity to speak to the thug.

Randy was attacked, choked, beaten, kicked and ridiculed for his faith. The guards turned deaf ears and blind eyes to what was taking place. They didn't believe that he'd changed, and the more he tried to explain to them, the less favor they granted him.

He didn't retaliate or turn in those who had mistreated him. Following what he'd read in the Word, he was given the strength to be able to 'turn the other cheek' in the face of his attackers.

Instead, he just followed orders without so much as a question, even when they were beyond what should be asked of him. Eventually, the others left him pretty much alone. He tried not to interact with them, and they avoided him like the plague.

Consequently, the Word and prayer became Randy's constant companions.

A few of the others began to watch him more closely to see if he was for real. But his consistent walk, though not easy on the inside, was quite evident on the outside.

As he finally ran out of memories of the worst days of his life, he again turned his future over to the One Who he knew would be there for him, no matter what. With that, he fell into a peaceful sleep, grateful that he had nothing to hide or to regret.

★ ★ ★

The rest of the week went by in a blur as Randy anticipated seeing Gerry. He wanted to hear about her presentation to the school board members. Did she get any good responses? She seemed so at peace, yet so lively. She had shared some of her life with him when they talked over tea at the bakery. Now, he wanted to know everything about her.

His boss, Fred, noticed Randy's ever-present smile all week. "What's got you so wound up? Is it a girl? It *is* a girl, right? I can tell."

"How can you tell? I mean, what girl?" Randy stammered.

"It's a girl alright. Nobody goes around smiling all the time unless they're in love, or on the way to it. So who is she? Have I met her? Tell me more," questioned his nosy mentor.

Truth be told, Fred had taken on the role of a father-figure as well as a mentor for Randy. Since Randy's dad had died when he was young, he'd lost out on having someone to talk to about the important things of life. His mom tried, but it just wasn't the same. Maybe that was why he had gotten into trouble.

"What makes you think it's a girl?" Randy kept smiling as he said this. Then he continued, "Well, yes, it *is* a girl. Rather, a young woman."

"I knew it! So, 'fess up."

"Her name is Gerry Smart. She's a school teacher. She came in a couple of weeks ago to place a large order for a big meeting where she and her co-workers were going to present programs to help underprivileged kids. We got to talking and found out that we're both committed Christians. There's just something about her that intrigues me. I want to get to know her more."

"Go on," the happy bakery urged.

"We're going out Friday night for something to eat and then attending a program at my church. That's all. For now."

"For now. If I know you at all, it won't be the last time you see her, right?" Fred joked.

"If we hit it off on Friday, I do hope that we can see more of each other. She's really pretty, but not in a forced kind of way. It comes from within. Her smile lights up her face."

"Oh, you've got it bad!" laughed his boss.

"Yeah, I kinda do," admitted Randy.

Sobering a bit, Fred said, "I'll be praying for you, son. It's time you found a good woman and settled down. Let me know how it goes on Friday."

"Thanks, Fred. I appreciate all your prayers. I don't want to get ahead of myself, or God, but am hoping that this could lead to something greater," Randy replied.

★ ★ ★

As Randy parked in front of the small house where Gerry lived, he took a deep breath as he moved up the sidewalk. *Lord, You know that I've been praying all week for tonight. Give me some sign that You approve of this relationship, if there is to be one. I don't want to go any further if You are not in agreement here. Thanks.*

Knocking on her door, Randy stepped to the side a little so as not to appear too eager. While he waited, he took in the sight of the various flowerpots on the porch, and the tinkling wind chime. He could see her touch everywhere. When Gerry opened the door, he nearly gasped. *She is so beautiful.*

"Hi, Randy, come on in. I'm almost ready," Gerry said as she opened the door wider.

Entering the neatly decorated living room, Randy could see some of her homey touches in the décor. The furnishings were contemporary without being ultra-modern. It gave off the impression of peace and tranquility. A few splashes of red here and there were eye-catching but not distracting.

"Please, have a seat. I really am ready, just need to add my earrings and I'll be all yours for the evening," she said, before realizing what those words might imply. With a somewhat red face, she headed down the hall to finish her preparations.

To Randy, she was just right. No amount of jewelry could add to her already attractive exterior. Without a doubt, she was just as pretty on the inside.

Once she was satisfied with her appearance, Gerry and Randy descended the stairs to his car. After opening her door for her and making sure she was safely inside, he walked around to the driver's side and slid in. "You look lovely tonight," he commented as he fastened his seatbelt.

"Why, thank you, kind sir. How splendid of you," she said in her best English accent.

They both laughed. This was starting out to be a very enjoyable evening.

CHAPTER 9

Once they were seated at the diner, and their drinks and food ordered, Randy opened up the conversation. "So, tell me about your meeting. How did it go? Did you get any encouragement or endorsements for your ideas? What now? I'm full of questions," he said, smiling.

"Thank you for your interest, Randy. That means a lot to me. Most of my friends think I'm on a fool's errand trying to convince staid educators with new ideas."

Randy replied before she could go on, "Don't ever let anyone tell you that you can't do something that God has said you can do!"

"Yes, sir!" She said, saluting him. "Anyway, the meeting was moderately successful. I've taught for so long I was beginning to wonder if these ideas would ever see the light of day. At least half of the board members came to me after the gathering and said that they would support whatever my friends and I wanted to do."

"That's great. I'm proud of you!" Randy said before realizing that they hardly knew each other and were just beginning a friendship. But he really was happy for her success.

"As to 'now what,' I have to find the funding to put the programs in place as well as the volunteers and staff to carry out the venture."

"That's something to pray about, isn't it?" he asked.

"You've got that right. I've been praying for favor with those who will see our vision. To know that more than one or two can see where I'm going is so rewarding."

"From the ideas you showed me a couple of weeks ago, I'm sure that this is only the beginning for you. I predict that soon a whole new program, even a building, will be named for you!"

"You are good for my ego! I appreciate your vote of confidence in me. God is the One Who gives me the ideas. We just have to tweak them until they feel right. I'm having a great time, even if I don't know where all of this will lead," confessed Gerry.

"Aren't you glad that God only gives us one day at a time? We'd probably run and hide if we knew all that He had in store for us," Randy replied.

Nodding and taking a sip of her iced tea, Gerry continued. "We've already contacted several of the business owners near the school to see if they will come along side my fellow teachers to implement the first phase of the program. Am I crazy?" she asked.

"No, not at all. Go for it! It's your dream. You'll never know if it will work unless you try," Randy encouraged.

Their food arrived, and following a blessing by Randy, they started on their main courses. As she was politely enjoying her grilled chicken, Randy couldn't help taking in the sight before him. Not only was she smart, and pretty, but she also had a secure faith in her Savior. Had God been keeping her in the wings for him all along? Only time would tell.

Breaking into his musings, Gerry said, "So, tell me, how you became a baker? If you'll pardon me for saying so, you don't look like a baker."

"Thanks, I think. I told you a little about my past life, how I left home when I was seventeen. I found out quickly that living on the streets is not the way anyone should live. Since I had not gotten my high school diploma before I took off, it was very difficult to get any job worth having.

"A guy I met somewhere—I don't even remember where—took me under his wing for a time. He encouraged me to take my equivalency test for a certificate. After that, jobs were a little easier to come by. However, none of them paid much more than minimum wage, if that," he admitted.

After a few bites of his meatloaf, he continued, "Anyway, I was ripe for the picking when this guy drives up beside me in a fancy car and says, 'Get in.' Even though I could tell he was wearing a fake beard and mustache, it was better than being out in the cold. He made me an offer I couldn't resist. And he paid me some decent bucks."

Gerry was thoughtful before she asked, "Didn't it seem odd to you that he was driving a luxury car but needed someone to do what he asked of you?"

"I didn't ask questions. He never told me his name. He said to call him *Boss*. All I could see were dollar bills with my name on them. He even got me a menial job and a place to live in a run-down boarding house. He paid me well for my expertise."

After a few more minutes, Gerry asked, "So, how did you get caught?"

"After a short while, I figured that since I was successful working for him, I could do the same thing for myself on the side. To me, his vision was short-sighted.

"But, I got too caught up in the game. I wanted more and better things. By the time I had acquired a good deal of money, I decided to deposit some of it in a bank. The bank managers had been advised to keep a watch out for anyone depositing a large amount of cash.

"Unbeknownst to me, I left a thumb print on the pen used to open the account. Since I'd been arrested a couple of times in the past for minor offenses, my prints were on file. After that, it was only a matter of time."

Gerry agreed, "I think I can understand what you mean. When you taste having money, and what it will buy, you can lose all sense of reason.

"I don't make that much as a school teacher, and could sure use an influx of cash, but I think I'll let the Lord be the One to give it to me in His good time."

Nodding, Randy added, "I wish I had known then what I know now. Ill-gotten gain never satisfies. But working for something brings far more pay than money."

Following their simple dinner and more getting-to-know-you conversation, they headed to Randy's church for the evening program. *I could get used to this*, Randy thought as he led this lovely lady into the sanctuary. *Please, God, don't let me get ahead of You. May Your will be done.*

Once they settled in their seats, Randy pointed out several of the people around them who had been great mentors to him since he had returned home. He spotted his mom across the room and motioned for her. She made her way over to where they were seated.

"Mom, I'd like to introduce Gerry Smart. Gerry, this is my Mom, Sally."

The two women shook hands at first before Sally drew her into a hug. Gerry returned the gesture with a hug of her own.

"So nice to meet you," Sally said. "I understand that you know my dear friend, Joan?"

"Oh yes, she's such a blessing to me, and to the others in our class at church. I've learned so much from her," Gerry said.

"And so have I. I don't know where I'd be if it weren't for her faith and friendship. I thank God often for her insight and abiding trust in Him."

As the women talked a bit longer, Randy just watched the interaction between them. It seemed obvious he wouldn't have to convince his mom of Gerry's sincerity. Both women had huge smiles on their faces.

"Randy, you must bring Gerry to dinner on Sunday," Sally commented.

Gazing at Gerry with a question on his face, she just nodded in his direction.

Just then the Pastor stepped up to the mic to introduce the evening's program. With a wave, Sally walked back to her seat with a grin and a nod of her head. Her son had very good taste. *Lord, please lead him in this new relationship. I know he wants Your will above all else. Guide both of them to know just what that is,* Sally prayed as she sat down to enjoy the program.

CHAPTER 10

Saturday could not come fast enough as Jenny Chambers anticipated the celebration of her Great Aunt Harriet's 90th birthday.

On Friday, Jenny and her mom, Kathleen Leonardi, were going to decorate the church fellowship hall for the great event. It wasn't just every day that someone reached such a milestone! She only hoped that she could be as 'with it' as her great aunt, if she lived that long.

When Jenny was a young girl, her parents, Kathleen and Joseph Reynolds, had sent her to her great aunt Harriet's for two weeks every summer. Jenny thought at the time that it was for her enjoyment. It really was for her parents to try to repair their fractured marriage. When Joseph died, Jenny's visits stopped.

She had missed those times of pure joy with the older woman. Harriet's husband, Grant Reynolds, had died many years prior to her visits. The couple had been childless, but that didn't stop Harriet from treating Jenny with all the love and fun she had missed bestowing on her own offspring.

Many times, Jenny would uncover great treasures in the attic, while Harriet regaled her with stories that were related to the various dresses, hats, and gloves that were unearthed. It seemed Harriet enjoyed the reminiscing as much as Jenny as she relived the times associated with each of the items.

Harriet's life had been filled with many community activities, including the garden club, the book club, Sunday school and church, as well as a weekly Bible study that she taught for many years. But, as she began to feel her age, one by one she stopped most of her outings until church on Sunday and a weekly trip to the beauty parlor were just about all that were left.

Her mind still stayed sharp for a woman of her advanced years. Jenny and Todd enjoyed visiting with her on several occasions. Harriet was even instrumental in the capture of a couple of phone scammers who tried to bilk her out of her money. Only the Lord could have orchestrated the events that lead to Harriet's bringing to the Lord the young woman, Janetta Willis, arrested for the crime.

For several months, Harriet had been mentoring both the girl and her mother, Blanche DuPree, in their newfound faith. With her gentle instruction, the two of them were growing quickly in their relationship with their Savior.

Jenny's thoughts returned from thinking about Aunt Harriet to tasks at hand. Grabbing her check list, she made sure all the arrangements had been covered: invitations sent, food ordered, flowers ordered, background music chosen, and decorations ready to put in place.

Harriet had insisted that she didn't want any fuss made over her, but Jenny and Kathleen paid her no mind. Her influence on dozens of people during her long life would be extolled by various speakers when the time was given for acknowledgements. Gifts were declined in favor of donations to one of Harriet's favorite charities.

Just then, the phone rang. "Hello," Jenny answered.

"Hi, honey. Just checking to be sure everything is ready for Saturday," Kathleen replied.

"I think we've covered everything. I'm so excited to honor Aunt Harriet like this. She is such a special lady."

"Yes, she certainly is. I'm only sorry I didn't realize that earlier in my life. I might have been brought to the Lord much sooner through her gentle witness," Kathleen acknowledged.

Jenny agreed, "I know what you mean. She tried to tell me about Him when I was small, but it just sort of went in one ear and out the other. When I finally accepted Jesus as my Lord and Savior, many of the things she had said began to make sense."

Kathleen added, "I'm sure her prayers had something to do with both of us recognizing our need of Him."

"No doubt about that. I just can't imagine my life without her in it. Her wisdom and patience, her sense of humor and knowledge of the Word are irreplaceable."

"Let's hope we have many more years to enjoy her before she's called home."

Jenny responded, "Yes, many, many more."

★ ★ ★

The decorating on Friday went by quickly, and Saturday morning dawned bright and clear. Even though Harriet's birthday was actually on Wednesday, this was the best day to have a celebration so more people could attend.

By the time Jenny's husband, Todd Chambers, brought Harriet to the hall, it had begun to fill up with dozens of people who loved this remarkable woman.

A special chair had been decorated like a throne, and it was to this that Todd carefully led the woman of the hour.

"Oh, my, I feel like a queen getting ready to view my subjects," joked Harriet.

"To us, you are a queen," Todd replied as he helped her to be seated. "May I bring you some punch, m'lady," he asked the monarch.

"That would be so nice, thank you kind sir," Harriet replied with a smile.

Soon she was surrounded by many friends, from her club activities, church, Bible study, and neighbors. It seemed she affected everyone she met in some way. Even the cab driver who transported to her hair appointment every week was there to help celebrate.

While the guests were enjoying the delicious food provided by the caterer, folks began extolling Harriet's many virtues.

"I remember when my husband died, I thought I could not go on," said an elderly woman. "But Harriet's kindness and understanding helped me get through those days of loss and bewilderment. I couldn't have made it through without her!"

"She is always so kind to me when we go to her beauty appointment each week," Artie, the cabbie related. "We talk about my family, my health, and my problems. She is so thoughtful to tell me she is praying for me," he said with tears glistening in his eyes. "I can't wait to see her every week. She brightens up my day and makes my job so much easier. She never complains or talks about herself. What a remarkable lady!"

The comments were many and the accolades numerous as one after another of Harriet's friends, neighbors, and fellow believers shared the things about Harriet that they appreciated the most.

Janetta Willis took the mic and began her speech, "I sure couldn't believe it when I started getting mail from Harriet while I was in prison for trying to talk her out of some of her money. Then, she actually drove all the way to visit me. It was the day that changed my life. She introduced me to my Savior, and my life has not been the same ever since," she finished with a smile and tears trailing down her cheeks.

Next up was Blanche DuPree, Janetta's mother. She began, "After being reunited with Janetta, and seeing how she had been affected by Harriet's visit, I wanted to know more. Now, Harriet is mentoring both of us in this walk with Jesus. Without her, I don't think either of us would be as happy and contented as we are," she said, smiling at her daughter, who just nodded in agreement. "Thank you, Harriet, for praying for us, and not giving up on a couple of used-to-be losers. We love you more than we can say." With that, Blanche also dissolved into tears.

Jenny shared some of her fondest memories from her childhood visits with her beloved aunt. "I must tell you the significance of the green pin that I'm wearing. It was a gift from Harriet to me for my high school graduation. Because of the theft and subsequent discovery of the pin, I met my husband, Todd, the police detective who came to investigate the break-in at my apartment. Thank you, Aunt Harriet, for providing just the thing that brought this unbelievable man into my life."

Harriet just nodded with a wink and wide smile on her face.

Then, Todd stood to share his own thanks. "It was such a delightful discovery when Jenny and I were first dating to find out that my late grandmother, Sadie Michaels, and Harriet had been best friends when they were young. Unfortunately, I lost my grandmother to dementia and death when I was a little boy. Aunt Harriet has more than filled that empty place I didn't even know was there. I couldn't love her more if she were actually a blood relative," he said, smiling at the teary-eyed woman.

Finally, it was Harriet's turn to speak. Todd helped her to rise from her 'throne' and move to the mic stand. Placing the instrument in her hands, he sat next to her in case she needed him.

Dabbing at her eyes, Harriet heaved a huge sigh, and then began, "You all will never know what this day means to me. I love each and every one of you because you have all made my life worthwhile. After my darling, Grant, passed on, I couldn't see any use for my life. But, God let me know right quick that He wasn't through with me yet. He wouldn't let me wallow in my sadness for long. Soon, He had me giving out to others, and in so doing, my grief began to fade. Yes, I still miss my man, and I can hardly wait for the day when we shall be together again. But I don't begrudge myself one single day that the Lord has allowed me to stay here.

"God has proven Himself over and over that He needs me for some reason, or else I would be outta here! I suppose I could give a sermon about now, but I will restrain myself!" This brought laughter from everyone.

"To live for ninety years was never something I thought would be my lot in life. But to tell the truth, I have enjoyed nearly every day of it. Seeing so many of you who mean so much to me makes me realize that I just might have been doing what God wanted for me all along. Thank you so much for all the kind words, the memories, and love that I feel today. There are not words to express my gratitude for knowing and loving all of you." Throwing kisses to everyone, Harriet reached for Todd's arm as he led her back to her seat.

★ ★ ★

By the time Harriet was home, the people disbursed, and the hall restored to order, Jenny and Kathleen declared it a very successful day.

"I'm so glad we did this," Jenny replied with a tired sigh.

"Me too," Kathleen agreed. Then they said in unison, "I hope to be just like Aunt Harriet when I grow up!"

Chapter 11

Babysitting for her grandson, Lyle was always a joy for Joan. Her son Philip and his wife Penny were taking a much-needed long weekend vacation before the birth of their second child. Joan relished the time she could spend with this special little guy.

Reading to him, helping him to sound out words, and identifying the pictures on every page showed off his quick and alert mind.

When he was younger, she would ask, "What does the horse say? What does the cow say? What does the cat say?" Just as quickly he answered each one with a hearty reply, "neigh," "moo," "meow."

He was now getting ready for kindergarten. Where had the time gone? She attributed his knowledge with the fact that Penny spent a great deal of time with him, teaching him things that he would need to know when he entered school.

Joan was sure that would change with the addition of another sibling. Penny was a great mother, so she would certainly find the time to spend with both of her children. The first one, however, usually received the most of his parents' time before having to share with anyone else. Penny had been getting Lyle ready for the newcomer.

The Good Path

He would be a great helper to her now that he was at the age where he still wanted to get involved. Since they knew that it was another boy, Lyle was already planning which of his toys he would share, and which ones he would keep just for himself. Of course, by the time the new baby was ready for those, Lyle would no doubt have out-grown them anyway.

"Grandma, can we go to the park?" asked the adorable, blue-eyed munchkin.

Smiling, Joan replied, "Yes, I think that can be arranged. How about we have some lunch first? Or, do you want to have a picnic instead?" she asked, already knowing the answer.

"Can we? That sounds like fun. Please, please, please," he pleaded.

Laughing, Joan assured him that they could do just that. With his help, she made peanut butter and jelly sandwiches, sliced some fruit into a container, and grabbed a couple of juice boxes. Placing everything into a backpack, she said, "Let's go," reaching for his hand.

The park was an easy walk two blocks from the house. It was a beautiful, spring afternoon, with sun shining brightly, flowers coming into bloom, and birds chirping their greetings along the way.

Finding just the right table for their banquet, Lyle said, "Here's the perfect spot," as he led Joan to a table near the swings.

"What makes this the perfect spot," she said, laughing at his earnest expression.

"I don't know, it just is," he answered.

"Okay, if you say so," she said as she spread a small cloth on the table before taking out their food and utensils.

Before she could even say anything, he took her hand and said a blessing on the food, "Thank you, God, for this food. Amen. Oh, and thank you for the hands that prepared it. Amen again."

It warmed Joan's heart to know that he was being brought up to honor the Lord. If only more children had that opportunity, the world would be a much different place. She prayed that he would hold on to his faith for as long as he lived.

Being all boy, Lyle scarfed down his food in a hurry so he could go take his turn on the swings. The playground had gotten a bit more crowded since they arrived, with several children vying for the four swings, the slide, and the merry-go-round. That didn't seem to deter Lyle. He just walked up to the line and waited his turn for the next available swing. Joan marveled at his quiet temperament. Somehow, he had learned to show restraint when he wanted so very badly to do anything.

After a few minutes of waiting, a swing became available. "Push me, Grandma," he yelled.

By this time, Joan had cleaned the table of their lunch items, depositing the trash in a nearby garbage can. Shouldering her backpack, she walked over to give her favorite person a huge shove high into the air.

"Weeee," he yelled at the top of his lungs. "Higher, Grandma, higher."

After several more arm-stretching shoves, she returned to the picnic bench to watch him pumping on his own. A huge smile covered both their faces. His was from the sheer joy of flying high. Hers from the joy he brought to her heart.

Seeing that there was a line forming for turns on the swings, Lyle gradually slowed to a stop, hopping off and running to the monkey bars. They were low enough that he had no trouble jumping up to grab a bar and swing across just like the primate for which it was named.

His energy level seemed to increase with each activity. Soon, he was off to the slide; then he tried the merry-go-round. Finally, he returned to Joan and flopped down on the ground at her feet, sagging as if he were worn out.

"That was fun. Let's go home now," he said, matter-of-factly.

Joan smiled at his comment, knowing that he would not admit to being tired, but was ready to call it a day.

They walked slowly back to the house, with Joan pointing out interesting rocks, bugs, and flowers to her inquisitive grandson. He reveled in her undivided attention. There was no such thing as spoiling your grandkids if you were giving them what they needed when they needed it. She wanted him to know that he was distinctive because God had made him just the way He wanted him.

When they entered the house, Lyle headed for his favorite spot in the living room. Instead of parking in front of the TV, he chose his small chair and a pile of books beside it. Picking up one about trains, he was soon engrossed in the easy story and pictures. Under his breath Joan could hear him sounding out the words, reading to himself a story he had heard many times. She wasn't sure if he was reading or reciting what he remembered. Either way, the words and the sounds would make a connection soon enough. To her, he truly was a unique little boy.

Joan unloaded the backpack and started fixing dinner. It would take a while for the potatoes to bake in the oven. The hamburgers were ready to broil when the time was right. She chopped some vegetables for a salad, and sliced some sourdough bread for toasting.

Then, she went back into the living room to read for a little while until the potatoes were done. Lyle had already made it through his pile of books. Now, he was making something with his blocks. She enjoyed watching the creativity at work as he would place a block, then make sure it was just so before adding another. Maybe he would be an engineer one day, or an architect. Whatever he chose, God was fashioning him for it even now.

After enjoying the simple dinner, with ice cream for dessert, Lyle again ran to his unfinished block creation. Soon, he had his small cars and people interacting in and around the structures. His imagination made Joan laugh silently. He was talking to the people, using different voices to distinguish each one.

"What is that you've made," Joan asked, her curiosity getting the better of her.

"It's a city where only kids live. But they can drive cars and have jobs and everything," he answered her as if it was obvious.

Rather than question him about it, she went back to reading her book until it was approaching bath and bed time.

"Okay, little man, it's time to get ready for going to sleep."

"Can I leave my city here, or do I have to put the blocks and everything away?" he asked hopefully.

"You can leave it just the way it is if you want. I won't touch it. It'll be right here waiting for you when you get up in the morning."

"Thanks, Gram, you're the greatest!" he exclaimed, running over to her and giving her a big hug.

Upstairs, he undressed while she drew his bath water. There were toys to play with while he was supposed to be getting clean.

"Don't forget to wash your face and ears," she said as she led him into the bathroom and into the tub."

"I won't, Gram, I'm a big boy now," he assured her.

"Yes, you are. But I will be holding an inspection when you finish just in case you forget."

"Okay."

Although she didn't sit and watch him, she did keep an eye on him from the hallway. Accidents in the bathtub were all too frequent. She didn't want him to become a statistic.

Soon, he was out, dried off, passed her eagle eye, and was dress for bed.

Kneeling beside his bed, he clasped his hands and said his prayers. "God bless Mommy and Daddy, and my new Brother. God bless Grandma, and my other Grandma and Grandpa, and God bless everyone everywhere," he said as he finished. "Oh, and God, bless my other Grandpa, wherever he is. Thanks, amen."

Joan had a lump in her throat as she tucked him in and kissed his forehead. Where had he come up with that last request?

"Good night, sleep tight," she said as she closed the door, leaving a small nightlight for him if he needed to use the bathroom during the night.

Retracing her steps to the living room, Joan ruminated over her grandson's last request. She had not mentioned Gary's unexpected visit a few weeks ago. Did he somehow find Philip even though she had refused to give him the information he demanded?

Maybe Philip had told him about his dad. But there wasn't much to tell since Gary had bailed out on them when Philip was still young. She wondered what Philip remembered. They rarely talked about those days that seemed so long ago.

Turning the matter over to the only One Who could make any sense out of it; she chose to leave it alone. If there was more to this than met the eye, it would come to light in God's good time.

Chapter 12

"Mom, I've got something to tell you," Philip said to Joan as they finished the Sunday dinner she had prepared.

"What is it, son? You can tell me anything, you know that."

As if gathering his strength, Philip went on, "I saw Dad a couple of weeks ago."

Joan could not have been more shocked. She had not given Gary any information as to where Philip was. How could he have found him?

Realizing that the news was a shock, Philip continued, "He called me out of the blue and wanted to meet. I couldn't figure out why, now, after all these years. He's made no contact since I was about eight years old, when he left."

Joan waited for him to continue. She could tell he was having a hard time sharing this bit of information with her.

"We met for coffee on a Tuesday, after I got off work. I was surprised that he seemed so old! I guess I expected him to look the same as the day he left. Anyway, we had a somewhat stilted conversation."

Not being able to help herself, Joan asked, "What did he want? What did you talk about?"

Philip took a drink of iced tea before he told his tale. "He wanted to be a part of my life."

"What? Why now, after all these years?" Joan couldn't keep some of her anger out of her voice.

"That's what I asked him. He said that he didn't want to miss any more of my life. He wants to meet Lyle and be a part of his life too. I asked him where he'd been for the last twenty years, but he didn't answer me."

Joan responded, "I didn't tell you this, but a few weeks ago he came to see me. He wanted information on how to find you. He seemed, so….hard, angry. I decided not to give him what he demanded. He stormed out of my apartment with a dark glare. I guess he used some other means to find you."

"Yeah, I kinda got the impression that life hasn't been all that great for him over the years. He not only looked old, he had sort of a haunted expression like he was dead inside. There was no life in his eyes like I remember when I was small. Back then, he used to laugh so much and his eyes had sparkled when we were together."

Carefully, Joan asked, "Did he tell you anything about his life, where he's been, what he's been doing?"

"No. In fact, when I asked, he shook me off without so much as a hint. He's definitely not the same man I remember."

They both chewed over this turn of events before Joan couldn't help asking, "Will you see him again?"

Philip said, "That's what he wanted, but I was hesitant. I don't need anyone in Lyle's life to upset him. And that's what I felt Dad would do. I told him I'd pray about it. He didn't like my answer one bit. He went off on a rant about you, church, prayer, the whole works. I just got up and left. We don't need this in our lives."

Sighing, Joan added, "I can't imagine what has happened to the fun-loving, gentle man that I married all those years ago. He was always laughing, making jokes, wanting to have fun. Then, when Julie needed so much attention, I think he felt left out. I tried my best to split my time between all three of you, but I don't think he even tried to understand."

They went on talking for a few more minutes while Penny cleared the table, and worked quietly in the kitchen, knowing that the whole situation had Philip in turmoil. Her prayers for him had helped, some, but he seemed to be a hurting little boy again, feeling once more rejected by his father.

Finally, Philip asked Joan, "What should I do, Mom? I'd like for Lyle to know his grandfather, but not the man I saw the other day. Should I talk with Dad again? Try to find out if he has something else driving him that brought him out of the woodwork now?"

Taking her son's hand, Joan said, "I know you've already prayed about this. What do you feel you are being led to do? Has God given you any insight or answers?"

Squeezing her hand, Philip replied, "Yes, I have prayed, and no, I don't know yet what to do. That's why I wanted to talk with you. You have so much wisdom I thought you could help me through this."

Not having any more insight than her son, Joan bowed her head and took the matter to the throne, "Father, You know all things. Only You can give us wisdom on what to do here. You've been with Gary for the last twenty years so You know just what he needs. We need Your direction on what to do next. Do we let him back into our lives, hoping we can have a good impact on him for You? Or, do we cut the remaining ties? We need Your help, Lord. Show us Your plan. In Jesus' Name, amen."

Mother and son sat quietly with their own thoughts, believing that they would receive instructions on how to handle this situation.

After several minutes, Joan replied, "I think I need to talk with him again. Maybe I can get to the bottom of this. Would that be okay with you?"

"Sure, Mom, do whatever God tells you to do. For me, I think I'm just supposed to wait and see. I remember long ago a Sunday school teacher telling our class: if in doubt—don't. I won't do anything until I know for sure it's the right thing to do."

Philip gave Joan the phone number Gary had given him.

At this point, Penny returned to the table with a pitcher of iced tea. "Refills, anyone?" she said with a smile. She could see that the lines around Philip's eyes had eased. Whatever was ahead, she would support her husband's decisions.

After her family left, Joan walked to her recliner and picked up her Bible. This situation was something that needed divine help. She had learned over the years that doing things in your own strength, with your own agenda, never worked in the long run. She was reminded of the scripture that said to trust God with all your heart and to not lean on your own understanding.

Right now, she had no idea what she would say or do if she and Gary met. But of one thing she was sure, when she needed it, God would give her the words and the compassion that were necessary.

CHAPTER 13

Greg Preston walked into the bar he hadn't frequented for over ten years. For the last six, he'd been in prison for a phone scam he and his girlfriend, Janetta Willis had pulled. Only good behavior got him out before his full sentence of ten years had been completed. *I must be living under a lucky star* he thought when he was told he'd be released early.

Spotting his old compatriot, Roberto, he headed over to his table. Greg had done some work for him several years before he had to go away.

"Hey, Roberto. What's up?" he said with a bravado he didn't quite feel as yet.

"Hey, man, where have you been? Haven't seen you 'round for a long time," commented the dark-haired, rather well-dressed man.

"I've been out of town," Greg said. No need to tell this guy where he'd really been. None of his business. He continued, "So what's going on man? Anything I can get in on?" asked the recently-released con.

"What kinda things you talking about, compadre?" asked Roberto with curiosity in his eyes.

"Oh, you know, something to make a little dough. I'm kinda short right now," offered Greg, taking a seat at the table.

"What do you mean, 'what's goin' on'? You haven't been around when I needed you, my friend."

"I told you. I've been out of town," Greg said angrily. Then, he tamped down his temper. More calmly, he said, "Ya know where I can make a bit o' cash, or a score, if you know what I mean."

"Yeah, I know what you mean, boy. Don't play coy with me. You look like you haven't had a square meal in a while," he observed.

He wasn't about to tell his old comrade that life outside had been hard in the six months since he'd been released. Nothing he tried netted him enough money to eat regularly, let alone pay for a place to live. He must be losing his touch.

He didn't want to admit that he needed this guy who had stiffed him more than once on their previous schemes. But, there was nowhere else to turn. He couldn't find any of the other guys who had provided ideas for getting easy money. He found out that a couple had died in deals gone wrong. One was in drug rehab—again. Another one was in prison for killing his girlfriend in a heated rage.

"Okay, let's not waste time beating 'round the bush. I need some cash and I need it now. Can you help me, or hook me up with someone who can, or not?" Greg replied with a little more anger than he knew would help him in getting what he wanted.

Roberto snubbed out what was left of his cigarette and faced Greg. "Okay, okay, don't get yourself all worked up. I was just trying to be friendly." He stood up and motioned for Greg to follow him.

That's more like it, thought Greg.

Roberto led Greg past the bar, through the curtain, and down a dark hallway. At the fourth door, he knocked and waited for an answer.

"Come," said the voice behind the door.

Walking into the room, Greg saw a bulky man seated at a desk. The ashtray overflowed with spent butts, and smoke was heavy in the air.

"Mr. Franzoni, this is my acquaintance, Greg. He wants gainful employment," said Roberto.

Motioning to Greg, he said. "Sit, sit. You may go now, Roberto."

"Yes, sir," said Roberto as he backed out the door.

"So, Greg, is it? How do you know Roberto?"

Sitting up straighter, Greg answered, "A few years ago he and I relieved some unsuspecting folks of their extra cash, so to speak."

"Ah, I see. So you are not hesitant to do what's necessary to increase your pocketbook. Is that right?" asked the large man. He was dressed in a suit, his tie slightly undone. His size said he could break Greg in two if he so much as looked at him crooked.

"Well, I'm not much into knocking people off if I can help it. But anything else that will get me some cash would be okay with me," replied Greg.

"Okay, I understand. No rough stuff? Or just no killing? Which is it?"

"Rough stuff I can handle, but I'd rather not do away with anybody. If that's alright with you."

The broad man replied, "Yeah, I think I can find you something to do that doesn't require such drastic measures. You done any breaking and entering? Any robbery? Like a bank or some other institution? Tell me about your experience, then maybe I can fit you with one or two of the jobs I have in mind."

Greg tried not to brag on himself about the scams and thefts that he had done before the last one got him arrested. He left that detail out of his litany.

"You ever been arrested? Jailed? In the joint?" asked Mr. Franzoni.

"Sure, hasn't everybody?" laughed Greg, hoping to not have to answer the question directly.

"Kinda smart-mouthed, aren't you? A simple yes or no would have been sufficient."

Swallowing his pride, Greg admitted, "Yes, sir. I've been arrested twice, the last time spending six years in the joint for a phone scam that went wrong. Got out six months ago. I've been in rehab more times than I can count. But I've stayed clean since I got out. Can't say that I wouldn't like to get hooked up again, but maybe I'd better try living without it for a while to see if I can make it."

Nodding, Mr. Franzoni said, "A wise choice. I like to have my employees clean. Otherwise, I can't trust them as far as I can throw 'em."

Scratching his chin, gazing over the desk at Greg as if sizing him up, he finally said, "Okay, here's what I'm gonna do." He went on to lay out a plan for Greg to join with a couple of other guys, unloading crates at a warehouse.

It didn't sound to Greg like it would make much money, but for some reason, he wanted to give the tough-appearing man the benefit of the doubt. Besides, it was his last hope. He'd tried everything he could think of to make money just to get by, but nothing had gotten him very far. Sleeping at shelters was getting old, quick.

Taking in his appearance, the big guy also told Greg where he could bunk while he was waiting for bigger and better things to come along.

It was like he was reading his mind!

With the address of the warehouse stuffed in his dirty jeans pocket, along with the name of his contact, Greg thanked his new employer.

Nodding to Roberto on his way out of the bar, Greg felt like maybe the tide had finally turned for him. At least, he was hooked up with someone who knew where to find him work that would result in cash in his pocket. He knew that he'd be sharing some of his pay with Mr. Franzoni, but something was better than nothing. At this point, he was willing to do whatever the guy asked, as long as it made him some dough.

★ ★ ★

Heading down the street to the address he'd been given, Greg wondered what could be so important in those crates that a guy like Mr. Franzoni would be interested. Maybe he needed to just do his job without asking. The less you know the better in this business.

If truth were told, he didn't expect to stay long in this job. With some cash in his pockets, he'd find something better to occupy his time. But giving a paying job a try for a while was better than starving.

CHAPTER 14

The boarding house he'd been assigned to was not far from the warehouse. The room was clean but very shabby. Rent was reasonable if he made the money Mr. Franzoni had mentioned to him. Even one missed payment of rent and he'd be out on the street. That had been his existence for far too long, so Greg decided to be a little more careful where his earnings went. Rent first, then food. After that, well, he'd figure that out when the time came.

Greg had to walk the several blocks to get to his job. Finding the warehouse district was not all that hard, but finding the right one took a little more investigation. Finally, he located the number on the paper Mr. Franzoni had given him. He hunted for a guy named Scrapper as he'd been told. What a name! Maybe it said something about his identity. Greg wasn't about to get into any altercations with the guy. Just do the job and don't ask any questions. At least he had something to do and a place to sleep at night. For now, that was enough.

Coming around the corner of the building, Greg saw several guys hoisting crates of various sizes onto pallets that were then moved into the warehouse by small trucks.

Sizing up the various men working, he went to the one who seemed to be in charge.

"Are you Scrapper?" he asked.

"Who wants to know?"

"Mr. Franzoni sent me. I'm supposed to help move these crates around," answered Greg.

"Oh, well, that's diff'rent." He extended his hand to the newly-hired man and asked his name.

"Greg. Greg Preston."

"Okay, Greggie, here's what you do."

Greg wasn't sure he liked the new moniker, but decided that he'd deal with that later. He could set the guy straight after he'd proved his worth.

Taking him over to the rest of the crew, his new boss introduced him.

"This here is Greggie. He'll be working with you guys."

Turning to Greg, he said, "This here is Chief, Less—with two s's—and Snake."

Greg reached out to shake hands but when none of the others did the same, he returned his fist to his pocket. Trying to keep up with Scrapper's instructions, he also took in the odd assortment of men. Chief gave off the vibe that he could do some serious bodily harm if you got on his bad side. Less was definitely not a small man either. Snake had a huge tattoo of his namesake on his bulging arm. Greg had no idea how he was going to fit into this bunch. But he would have to do his best work. By the looks of the others, he'd be building up his own muscles in no time.

"Okay, boys. You're on your own," said Scrapper as he walked away.

"Well, well, well," said Chief. "What brings you to this part of town? You don't seem like a heavyweight. Are you sure you can handle the job?"

Before he could answer, Snake said, "Aw, leave the guy alone. Let's see what he can do before you count him out." Giving Greg the once over, he said, "You work with me today. We shift duties around as needed. Right now, we're unloading this shipment into the warehouse. Have you ever run a forklift?"

Greg swallowed. "No, sir, I haven't."

"Forget the 'sir' bit. My name is Snake. Just call me that, okay?"

"Sure, Snake. Okay. Show me what to do. I'm willing to learn," offered Greg.

The rest of the day found Greg running the forklift back and forth from the loading dock into the warehouse. There was no indication on the sides of the huge crates what they contained. He wasn't about to ask any questions at this point either.

By the time the day had ended, his muscles were as sore as if he'd spent the day in the gym. Not only did he run the forklift, but he also helped shove crates around that were too small for the machine, but not too small for a man to move. But they were heavy nevertheless.

With only a short break for lunch, which came from some vending machines in the back of the warehouse, there wasn't any time for a break. None of the guys brought a *brown bag* lunch. He'd have to make sure that he had enough change to get his daily food or he'd starve!

These guys didn't take any time to gab or even many smoke breaks. Instead, they worked like their tails were on fire. *They must know something I don't know*, thought Greg. He wondered what could be in those crates that was so important, and why weren't there any markings on them? Oh, well, if he was supposed to know, he'd find out. Otherwise, he'd just keep his questions to himself.

None of the guys seemed like they wanted to be all that friendly. For Greg, that was okay with him. He wasn't about to delve into his life story with any of them. He really wasn't all that interested in them either. Just do your job, keep your mouth shut, and collect your pay at the end of the week, he kept telling himself. This job was only temporary anyway. Just long enough to get some cash. Then he'd be off to bigger and better things.

★ ★ ★

About two weeks after beginning to work at the warehouse, he accidently let a crate slide off the forklift. You'd have thought he committed mass murder! The rest of the guys came running, yelling at him like he'd set the place on fire. What was the big deal? The crate only had a crack in the side panel. How could that hurt anything?

"What you think your doin'," yelled Chief

"Sorry, Chief. It slipped," replied Greg.

"This is valuable cargo. Something like that could get us all fired—or worse. You gotta be careful. Treat these babies like, well, babies. Got it?" Chief said with anger in his voice as he inspected the slightly-damaged crate. Satisfied that nothing had been moved out of place, he walked away, shaking his head. He turned around and said to Greg, "Strike one." Greg knew exactly what that meant.

What could be so valuable in those huge boxes that would set Chief into a sweat? Most of the crates only stayed in the warehouse overnight, or for a few days, before they were loaded into trucks or a huge semi to be taken who knew where.

Greg wondered if he could find out any information about the contents or if he should just mind his own business. Could the stuff be hot? Or illegal imports? Or what? Even though he knew that the guy who had hired him wasn't exactly a model citizen, he really didn't want to get involved in something that could send him back to the slammer. Maybe ignorance was bliss. Curiosity was said to kill the cat, and he had no intentions of becoming a feline.

CHAPTER 15

On a bright, sunny morning, the phone rang at the Chambers' residence.

Jenny scanned the caller ID and recognized the number as her great aunt Harriet.

"Hi, Aunt Harriet, how are you?" she asked with a smile on her face.

"Oh, Miss Jenny, this isn't Miss Harriet," said an anxious Rosaline, the young woman who cleaned Harriet's home twice a month.

"Hi, Rosaline, how are you today? You sound out of breath. Is everything okay?" asked Jenny with growing concern.

"Oh, Miss Jenny, it's awful, just awful. I came to clean Miss Harriet's home today…." Crying, she continued, "I found her asleep in her bed, which seemed so out of the ordinary. But I can't wake her up. I'm so scared. What shall I do?"

With heart pounding, Jenny asked, "Did you call 911?"

"I didn't do anything but call you," sniffled Rosaline

"Okay, Rosaline get ahold of yourself. Make the call and I'll be right there," she assured the distraught young woman.

"Okay, if you say so. But what do I do when they get here?" She asked, so frightened she could hardly speak.

Thinking for a moment, Jenny replied, "Just tell them what you told me, and when they arrive, show them to Harriet's room. I'll be there as soon as I can."

Softly, Rosaline responded. "Yes, ma'am." The phone went dead in Jenny's hand.

Jenny's son, Timmy, was in school until three, and daughter Abby was at pre-school. Quickly, Jenny called her mother, Kathleen.

"Mom, oh, thank God, you're home," she yelled into the phone.

"Jenny, what in the world is the matter? Has something happened to Todd?"

"Todd? Oh, no. It's Aunt Harriet. Rosaline just called and said that she couldn't wake her up. I told her to call 911 and I'd be right there. Can you pick up Abby at 11:30 and Timmy at 3 if I don't get back in time?"

Jenny had so many thoughts running through her head that she could hardly concentrate. What if she lost her beloved Aunt? How would she manage without her sage advice?

Relaxing her voice somewhat, Kathleen replied, "Of course, I'll be glad to pick up the kids. Don't worry about them. Go find out what's happened. Maybe Harriet just took too much of her medicine or something. Call me when you know more."

Grabbing her purse as she headed for the door, Jenny replied, "Thanks, Mom, I'll call you." Dropping the phone on the couch, she headed out the front door. *Not Aunt Harriet! I'm not ready to lose her. Please, God, not yet!*

It wasn't far to the large, older home in the once up-scale part of town where Harriet and Grant started their married lives. He had done very well in business, which was evident with the size of the house, the furnishings, and the generosity of her aunt.

Pulling up behind the emergency vehicle in the front of the house, Jenny ran up the steps into the arms of Rosaline, who was sobbing as if her heart would break.

Hugging her tightly, Jenny, looked into her eyes and knew without asking. "She's gone, isn't she?"

Nodding her head, Rosaline dabbed at her eyes with an already soggy tissue.

Jenny took a long breath, prayed for strength, and glanced up to see a man coming down the hall.

"Mrs. Chambers, I presume. I'm Dr. Thornton, the county coroner," he said, extending his hand.

Jenny limply shook it, trying to gather her rampaging thoughts.

"What happened?"

"I can't say conclusively without an autopsy, but I believe she just went to sleep and didn't wake up. There is no sign of trauma, no indication of overdose. It was probably just her age that finally caught up with her," he said kindly.

Still stunned, Jenny just nodded her head as she tried to accept the news.

"I will add," said Mr. Thornton, "when she passed on, she had a smile on her face."

"That sounds like Aunt Harriet. She probably got a glimpse of where she was headed and couldn't wait."

"I beg your pardon?"

"She saw her beloved Savior Jesus, and was more than ready to go be with Him."

"That explains a lot." Then he added, "I've wondered about that. Why do some folks leave with a grimace and some with a smile? I think you've just cleared that up for me. Thank you."

Jenny replied, "When our hope is in Jesus and what He's done for us, we are more than ready to go be with Him. Aunt Harriet lived her life praising, worshiping and teaching about the Savior Whom she loved with all her heart."

Reaching into his pocket, Dr. Thornton handed Jenny his card. "If you have any more questions, please don't hesitate to call."

"Thank you," she replied before asking, "What do I do now? What will happen to Aunt Harriet?" she could not bring herself to say her *body*.

"Do you know if Mrs. Reynolds had made any arrangements for when this eventually happened?" he asked kindly.

Taking a huge breath, Jenny answered, "Yes, she did. Let me go to the desk and get the folder."

Just a few weeks ago when she and Todd had been visiting with Harriet, the elderly woman had sat them down and gone over all the plans she had set in place. Jenny didn't really want to think about it, but the ever-practical ninety-year-old wasn't about to let her get away with that.

Harriet had admonished, "You know, dear, that the day will arrive. It's inevitable. I just want to ease your grief by not having to think about making any of the arrangements. Everything is taken care of ahead of time. Here's the name of the funeral home, the kind of service I hope you'd want for me, who should be the pallbearers, the songs, the music, everything.

"Just put it in motion, and it'll take care of itself. Everything is paid for so you don't have to worry about spending any of your money. I've already discussed this with my pastor, and my lawyer, so they know what to do as well. All the information is in this folder which will be in the top desk drawer when the time comes."

Jenny had put the thought out of her mind, hoping that she would not need the information for years to come. Now, before she was ready, it was here.

Going to the desk, she retrieved the folder, giving Dr. Thornton the name of the funeral home.

He said, "If you like, I can call them to pick up the bod…er, remains."

Jenny sighed, "Yes, thank you. That would be helpful."

Realizing that she had completely ignored Rosaline, she turned to the still upset young woman.

"Why don't you go home? I know this has been a great shock to you."

Rosaline was a college student who earned her spending money by cleaning a few homes during her breaks from classes. She had only been coming to Harriet's home for two years, but she had become one of Harriet's cherished ones whom she led to the Savior almost as soon as Rosaline started.

Sighing deeply, Rosaline stood from the chair where she had collapsed and grabbed Jenny in another fierce hug. "What will I do without her?"

Feeling the same way, Jenny just hugged back without comment. Right now there were not words to answer that question. Somehow, they would get through this, but only with God's help.

They both understood that they had known a very special person that was placed in their lives to lift them up closer to the God of Love. And they may never meet another like her again. She had loved deeper, prayed broader, hoped eternally, and taught divinely. What a treasure had been among them!

CHAPTER 16

The funeral for Harriet Reynolds was truly a celebration of a life well-lived. Nearly all of the people who had been at her birthday party only a few months before were now here to remember again how her life had touched theirs. Many more from the community who had been affected by her presence came to pay their respects, whether or not they actually knew her well.

The service was held at Harriet's church since the funeral home would never contain all of the people who wished to be there. The church was nearly full.

Todd, Jenny, Kathleen and her husband, Tony, as well as Timmy and Abby, were seated in the second row as one after another came to the stage to extoll Harriet's many ways in which she had gladdened lives.

"Hi, my name is Thelma Watkins. I was out walking my dog one afternoon, several years ago, when this spry little lady caught up with me. She said she was out for her 'constitutional' and wondered if I minded company. Little did I know when I agreed how she would impact my life," said the sixtyish woman.

"You see, just a few weeks prior to that, the love of my life had died unexpectedly. I felt so alone, like no one could possibly understand what I was going through. I was a nominal Christian at the time, and let me tell you, I was mad at God!" she said with a smile on her face as she mopped up tears.

Continuing, she added, "But that didn't throw Harriet off one little bit. The more we talked, the more I knew that her coming along was not a coincidence. We became friends, often having tea together, as she helped me through those difficult days. I don't know what I would have done without her. And, oh yes, I did commit myself fully to Jesus as a result because of her!"

There were tears flowing in the audience after Thelma spoke. Likely by many of those who had experienced those same surprise visits with Harriet.

Over thirty people shared similar stories of Harriet's influence in their lives. Age was not a factor as both young and old—and in between—claimed she had changed their lives. What a legacy the unassuming woman had left behind. Nearly everyone said they wished to be just like her when they grew up!

Jenny wiped tears from her eyes as she reveled in the testimonies of so many. If truth were told, nearly everyone in the sanctuary could share similar stories. There were tears, and there was laughter. How like Aunt Harriet. She would have loved this, but would quickly have given the credit to her Savior.

When it was her turn, Jenny walked to the microphone, the notes in her hand quivered as she took a breath before beginning.

"As many of you know, when I was young, I spent two weeks every summer with Aunt Harriet. We had so much fun! I didn't see her as some old relative on whom my parent's pawned me off. I found her to be childlike in her outlook on life. Nothing seemed to get her down, and she never made fun of my questions or childish behavior.

"The stories she told me about her early married life with Grant made me long to have the same kind of marriage one day. Even the almost 'love at first sight' they experienced when they first met was repeated in my life many years later.

"Her wisdom and advice when asked always seemed to be just what I needed at the time. It will be hard to not pick up the phone or go to her home to visit with her. Someone just told me this week that when you want your loved one who has died to know something, just tell Jesus, and He can tell that person! That gave me so much peace. All of us who know Jesus will be together rejoicing one day when we will be reunited."

After several more memories, Jenny turned the service back to the pastor who did an admirable job of summing up the life of the remarkable woman they were celebrating. He made sure that anyone who wanted to know more about this life of faith, and having Jesus as a personal Savior and Friend should come talk with him following the service.

Those who chose not to attend the gravesite, stayed at the church enjoying the light lunch that had been prepared. The line-up of cars going to the cemetery was nearly a half-mile long! Police escorts directed traffic to keep the honor of this wonderful woman unbroken by line breakers. Thankfully, it was less than five miles to the burial site.

The service lasted only fifteen minutes once everyone arrived. The pastor again laid out the plan of Salvation for those who might only have come to pay respects, but who did not yet know Harriet's precious Jesus. Three or four were seen talking with him following his kind words of comfort.

Meanwhile, Jenny greeted as many people as she could, inviting them back to the church for the luncheon. Most said they would return, but a few had to get back to work.

Jenny spotted Rosaline in the crowd and they immediately hugged each other tightly.

"How will I ever get along without her?" asked the teary-eyed young woman.

"Like the rest of us, one day at a time," offered Jenny with tears of her own. "One day at a time."

Chapter 17

Todd and Jenny Chambers, hands clasped, entered the lawyer's mahogany-walled office having no idea what the reading of Aunt Harriet's last will and testament would hold for them. Jenny's aunt had meant the world to her and she was still trying to adjust to life without the gentle, wise woman.

The sweet-smiling secretary took their names and motioned for them to have seats. She said, "Mr. Thornton will be with you shortly. May I get you something to drink? We have coffee, tea, and bottled water."

Trying to swallow, Jenny answered, "Bottled water sounds great. Thank you." Todd nodded his agreement.

When the cold, refreshing drinks were in their hands, Jenny leaned over to Todd. "We never talked about what Aunt Harriet planned to do with her house, or anything else. I can't even fathom that she's gone, much less think about disposing of her things."

Todd squeezed her hand and gave her a tender smile. "I know. She was such a remarkable lady. I miss her too. No matter what unfolds today, let's just try to 'go with the flow' if possible."

Soon, they were seated at a small conference table with several others already in attendance. Jenny recognized some of the faces as friends of Harriet's, or those who had done work for her. It would be just like Harriet to leave them each some small token of her appreciation. She was always thinking of others.

Mr. Miles Thornton, a sixty-something, brown-eyed and graying gentleman entered and took his seat at the head of the table. The kindly secretary came and sat at his right.

"Thank you all for coming. I'm sure Harriet Reynolds meant quite a lot to each one of you. We talked often of the people she cherished. I have been her lawyer for nearly forty years, and we shared a deep friendship as well as a lawyer-client relationship."

Gathering his composure, he continued. "Without further ado, let's get started." He read through the preliminaries of the will and then said, "Now, here is the part that affects each of you."

Everyone sat up a little straighter so as not to miss a word.

"To Miriam Hastings, my faithful hairdresser, I leave the sum of $15,000, to help you open your own shop." It was a good thing that several boxes of tissues were on the table as Miriam grabbed several and sobbed into them.

"To Artie Cole, my weekly ride wherever I needed to go, I leave the sum of $10,000, so you can take that lovely wife of yours on a romantic vacation."

Mr. Thornton remarked at this point, "Harriet wanted each of you to be blessed and to use the money as best suits you. She told me that both of you have blessed her each week with your faithfulness and friendship. She thought it was the least she could do."

Picking up the paperwork in front of him, Mr. Thornton continued, "To Thelma Watkins, my dear friend, I leave the sum of $20,000."

More tissues were handed down the table as tears cascaded down the older woman's face.

There were several smaller amounts given to others who were seated with the group, including Rosaline, Harriet's housecleaner; her gardener; the head of the book club; and her paper deliverer.

Mr. Thornton allowed each person some time to absorb the news before dismissing all but Todd and Jenny.

The secretary followed the beneficiaries to the front office where the particulars were handled as to receiving their checks.

Once the others had left, Mr. Thornton addressed Jenny, "As you know, or maybe you didn't know, Harriet Reynolds was quite wealthy. Her late husband, Grant, did quite well in business, and invested wisely. Harriet was frugal most of her life, especially after Grant died. She told me she had the Lord and that was all the wealth she needed. We had many conversations about her faith, and I'm happy to say, she led me to the Lord quite early on in our relationship. Of course, what she didn't leave to you and the others will be divided among her favorite charities and her church."

Jenny and Todd nodded in the efficient attorney's direction, still not having any idea what that dear lady had left for them. Jenny thought, *I had no idea Aunt Harriet was wealthy. I knew she had money, but can't even fathom the extent of it.* Butterflies in her stomach began doing a rumba as she sat up a little straighter. Could this mean that she and Todd would be able to have some extra to put aside for their children's education, maybe take a trip, or even move into a larger house?

Coming out of her musings, Jenny had to ask, "Say that again?"

Mr. Thornton replied, "Your aunt left you the bulk of her estate. The amount exceeds six figures, and it includes her house, her investments, and her bank accounts after the gifts to charities are disbursed." Pushing a piece of paper across the table in their direction, Todd and Jenny gasped at the enormous amount. Stunned, they had no words for several moments.

The kind lawyer just waited until the shock wore off before continuing. "You may use the funds as you see fit for your family. As you may well know, you are her only living relative. She loved you both, as well as your children, with an intensity borne from her loneliness."

At this statement, Jenny began to protest.

Holding up his hand, Mr. Thornton continued, "She had many friends and acquaintances, but there wasn't a time when we were putting all these things together that she didn't talk of you, Jenny, and brag how delighted she was when you and Todd met and married. Your children were the grandchildren she never had. I saw many pictures and heard many tales of their exploits!"

Sitting back in her chair, Jenny shook her head in wonder. Why had Harriet never told her what she planned? Of course, if she had, Jenny would have tried to talk her out of it, or persuaded her to give to more charities and others.

Jenny protested, "I never befriended Aunt Harriet again just so I could be remembered in such a dramatic way. It was never about the money. She had always been such a positive influence on me when I was a child. When our visits ceased after my father died, I really missed her."

"Yes, she knew that," replied Mr. Thornton. "She regaled me with stories of your visits and the fun you had with tea parties and old photo albums. I think she missed you more than you ever missed her. She told me that she had never stopped praying for you from the time you first went to visit her. When she learned that your intended was her old friend's grandson, it was like a double portion for her. It meant that she had both of you to love and enjoy."

After a pause, he resumed, "Did you know that she helped with your college education?"

"What?" asked an astonished Jenny?

"She swore the dean of the school to secrecy. You were given scholarships and tuition discounts because of her generosity. She never wanted you to know or to feel obligated to her in any way. She was so proud of the young woman you have become, as well in your role of wife and mother. If you had been her flesh and blood, she could not have been more gratified."

"Wow!" Todd exclaimed, lost for words. Up to this point, he had been trying to process the dollars represented on that piece of paper, and what they would mean for the future of his family.

"My grandmother, Sadie Michaels, loved Harriet as her best friend. My mother told me that she often mentioned her and the deep friendship they shared; and when grandma became senile, she would often talk to the Harriet of her memories.

"I wish there was some way to thank her for her generosity," Todd said with tears in his eyes.

Gently, Mr. Thornton took both their hands and said a prayer of commitment for them, that they would use this gift to not only provide for their family, but also for the needs of others. He concluded with thanks for the life that Harriet Reynolds had lived and asked that they could each live up to her memory.

Rising from their chairs, the young couple shook hands with the one representing their benefactor, and walked out to the front office. The well-prepared secretary gave them papers to sign, handed them the information on all of Harriet's accounts for which she had already added their names as beneficiaries, and then came around the desk to hug each one with tears in her eyes. "Your aunt was one very special lady. She led me to the Lord many years ago, and always asked about my family or any prayer needs. I will miss her greatly."

Nodding in agreement, Todd and Jenny walked out of the office in a daze with a sense of awe at what had just taken place. Only time would tell how those funds and provisions would affect their lives.

Reaching their car, Todd opened the door for his wife, and then went around it and got in. Before he could start the motor they both broke down sobbing. Neither of them had expected this! It was just too much!

Finally gathering himself together, Todd said, "Wow! I never saw that coming! Did you?"

Jenny wiped her face and answered, "No way! I thought a few thousand dollars, maybe, but nothing like this. I can hardly believe it. We're so blessed! I mean, we can pay for the kids' college, take a vacation, and so much more without having to always think about pinching pennies. I wish I could just hug Aunt Harriet right now. I knew she was special but this is beyond anything I would have ever imagined."

Todd added, "I've always heard about a 'rich uncle' dying and leaving you money, but I never expected it to be a rich aunt! I'm still in shock!"

Turning the key in the ignition, Todd pulled the car away from the parking space and headed home. They had a lot to decide. *Help, Lord,* he prayed.

Chapter 18

The wind blew through their hair as twins David and Dean peddled their bikes down the country road. Farms lined the way as they headed to their friend Josh's house.

An imposing black car with tinted windows sped past them, leaving a wake of wind and dust. Peering at the receding car, David yelled, "Wow, mister, slow it down. This is a two-lane, country road. Didn't you see the speed limit sign?"

Shaking his head, Dean added, "Those city guys never pay any attention! At least he moved over and didn't hit us. What's the hurry?"

David responded, "Man, I'm glad I don't live in the city. Nothing is that important that you have to risk your life or someone else's."

The boys had stopped as the car sped by, but now they continued their journey. It was only a mile from their farm to their friend's house, and they had traveled the distance many times. At twelve, the twins were hard-working, fun-loving tweens who enjoyed the peace and quiet of country living.

A few minutes later, in the distance, they saw the black car by the side of the road and almost felt justified in their assessment that the guy deserved to have car trouble.

Before they could get any closer, the driver dumped a huge bundle off the side of the road and then sped off.

Again, the boys stopped to watch. "I wonder why city folks think it's okay to dump their garbage way out here?" Dean commented.

Peddling their bikes closer, they scanned the black pile of garbage and were almost on their way again, when David spotted something.

He laid down his bike and walked a little closer to the edge of the road.

Carefully easing down the embankment, David grabbed a stick on the ground and poked at the object. He yelped when the item rolled further down the slant.

Racing back to his brother, he yelled, "It's a body!! We have to call the sheriff!"

Without asking any questions, Dean pulled his cell phone out and dialed the county sheriff's office. In this farming county, the only law officers were the deputies and the head man.

Nervously he asked for Sheriff Tate, stating that it was an emergency. Nancy Hildebrand, the only female deputy, asked who was calling. "It's me, Dean Grassley, and I have to talk to the Sheriff right away."

"Okay, okay, hold your horses, Dean. He's right here," Nancy said as she put him on hold.

"Hi Dean, what's up?" asked the man they knew as their Sunday school teacher as well as the representative of the law.

"Sheriff, we found a dead body. At least I think he's dead," Dean said with a hiccup in his voice.

"Whoa, wait a minute, son, back up and tell me what's going on. Where are you?"

"David and I are on state road 27 about half-way between our house and Josh Plummer's place. This big black car sped by us as we were about a quarter mile from home. Then we saw it stopped by the side of the road. Someone dumped out what we thought was garbage and then sped off, spewing gravel all over the place.

"When we got to the spot, David went and poked it with a stick. It rolled over, and it was….a body." Dean finished quietly. He and his brother had seen both life and death on their farm, but never anything like this.

"Okay, son, don't touch anything and wait where you are. I'll be right there," ordered Sheriff Tate, using his official voice.

The boys sat on the side of the road, not wanting to get any closer to what looked to be a man in a dark suit.

Soon, the county car came to a stop behind them, Sheriff Tate and a deputy exited and walked toward them.

The boys just pointed in the direction of their find.

Within minutes, the two men determined that the man was, indeed, deceased.

The deputy went back to the car and called for an ambulance and the coroner.

Meanwhile, the sheriff said to the two boys, "Did you get a good look at the car? Or the license plate? Just tell me everything you saw or remember. Can you describe the driver?"

Dean and David did their best to give whatever information they could, but it was minimal.

"Thanks for calling me. If you remember anything else, you know where to find me. Why don't you go on home? We can take care of things from here," he instructed them.

David asked, "When you find out who killed him, do we have to go to court?"

"We'll see. At this point, we have to find out how he died and when. Then we'll go from there. If I learn anything you need to know, I'll call you. Now, off with you. And thanks again."

The boys reluctantly got on their bikes and headed on to Josh's house instead of home. This was a story worth repeating, even if there wasn't much to tell.

Chapter 19

Kirk Walters rushed into Todd's office. "Did you see that the body those kids found in the country was Roberto Jenks?" he asked excitedly.

Todd raised his eyes from the print-out in his hand. "Yeah, I just read that! Can you believe it? That guy may have cheated prison, but now he's in a much worse place," Todd said, shaking his head. "Have they found out yet who did it, or where, or when?" He asked his fellow detective. "I've only just now begun to read the report and hadn't gotten that far."

"The medical examiner said that it was a single shot to the back of his head. Guess he never saw it coming. Nobody should be taken out like that," reflected Kirk. "As to when, it was probably within the last forty-eight hours; but so far, no idea where. Officers have already checked his fancy apartment, but there were no signs of any trauma," answered Kirk.

Todd sighed. "Looks like we have a job ahead of us, checking out all his haunts and hangouts. Didn't he frequent that bar down on third?"

Kirk nodded as he said, "Yeah. Best we start there. It'll be like finding a single four-leaf clover in a football field."

"All I can say is that God can bring to light what is hidden in darkness. We'll have to hold on to that promise if we're going to find the answer to this one," commented Todd as he rose from his chair and pulled on his jacket. "After you."

★ ★ ★

As Todd and Kirk walked into the less-than-upscale establishment, they surveyed the few occupants on their way to the bar. Identifying themselves and showing their badges to the bartender, Todd produced a former arrest picture of Roberto Jenks to the man and asked, "Have you seen this man before?"

Unbeknownst to the detectives, Roberto was a right-hand man to Mr. Big. Those who worked in the bar had learned the hard way that they had better stay on his good side, or pay the price.

The nervous wiping of the bar was a dead giveaway, but the barkeep answered, "I suppose I've seen him in here. I can't remember everyone who comes in. I don't have that kind of memory."

After several more questions, Todd asked, "Who's in charge around here?"

The guy continued wiping down the counter as he sized up the two detectives. With a sneer, he motioned towards a curtain in the back of the room. "You'll find him back there, fourth door." With that, he turned and walked away toward the end of the bar.

Under his breath, Kirk said, "Nice guy."

When they reached the correct door, Todd knocked loudly.

"Yeah, what do you want?" an angry voice answered.

"Police, we need to talk with you."

After some paper shuffling, they heard. "Come."

Again offering their badges and identifying themselves, Todd asked, "And your name is....?"

The large guy replied, "Franzoni." No other explanation was given.

Showing him the picture, Todd tried again. "Mr. Franzoni, are you familiar with this man by the name of Roberto Jenks?"

A quick smirk and then, "Yeah, so what?"

"How well do you know him? Are you friends? Does he work for you?" asked Kirk.

The big man just scoffed and said, "He comes in a few times a week. I don't get friendly with the clientele."

Kirk asked, "When was the last time you saw him?"

"How should I know? I don't check on the customers every night. I've got more important things to do," Mr. Franzoni said angrily.

"And what might that be?" asked Todd.

Mr. Franzoni stood so fast his chair hit the wall behind him and heatedly said, "I've told you all I know."

With a glance at each other, Todd and Kirk thanked him for his time and left.

On the way back to the precinct, Kirk commented, "He seemed quite scared didn't he? So did the barkeep. Like they didn't want to have anything to do with one Roberto Jenks or whoever killed him."

"Yeah, something doesn't add up here. Goes back to my theory that there's someone higher up than Roberto who must have ordered the hit. Wonder what he did to get himself eliminated. Those two back there sure don't want to end up the same way. Maybe we need to bring both of them in for further questioning. I'm not satisfied with any of their answers."

Kirk quickly agreed, and called ahead to have officers sent to the bar for the police escort to headquarters.

★ ★ ★

Mario Franzoni wrung his hands as he waited for Mr. Big to make time to see him. He'd heard how Roberto met his end and he wasn't about to become a similar statistic. He asked himself again and again how he had gotten himself mixed up with these people. As soon as the police detectives had left the bar, he was on the phone asking for an appointment with the one who ordered his footsteps. How could he have been so stupid to even admit that he knew Roberto? He was sure that the police would bring him in for more questioning and he needed a good alibi or excuse, quick.

Soon, he was ushered into the presence of the one who held so many lives in his hand. One word from this guy, and you were history.

"And what may I do for you today, Mario?" asked the well-dressed man on the leather couch. He didn't motion for Mario to be seated.

Mario had only been in these hallowed premises once before, and he barely made it out the door before he had to make a quick stop in the men's room.

Searching for the right words, he said, "Sir. The police came to the bar today, asking about Roberto. I didn't know what to tell them. All I said was that he was a customer and that I know who he was."

"Ah, so you know that Mr. Jenks is no longer with us," replied the man calmly.

"Yes, sir, I did hear that."

"And do you know why he is no longer among us?"

Again nervously, Mario replied, "No, sir."

Getting up from the couch, Mr. Big headed to the liquor cabinet on the far wall. Pouring himself a drink, he took a large swallow before turning to the anxious man.

"He decided that he knew more than I about how to handle this business. Do you think that was a smart move?"

Licking his lips trying to add some moisture to his already dry mouth, Mario just shook his head.

"Good. Now you understand. If you should be asked any more questions by the authorities, you will give them nothing. Do you comprehend what I'm saying?"

Again, a nodding of the head.

"Okay, let's just say that this was an unfortunate happening and get back to the business at hand. Just do your job, running the bar, sending me workers as they present themselves, and keeping your mouth shut. Think you can do that?" he asked with a threatening glare.

"But...." By the expression on Mr. Big's face, Mario stopped before he could say another word.

"That will be all." Mr. Big said as he left the room. Mario just stood there shaking, thankful that he was still alive. He didn't know what he'd do if he ever got on that man's bad side. He'd heard too many stories of people who just disappeared or ended up dead. He'd have to have his smarts about him if he expected to be able to stand up to any more inquiries from the authorities.

Maybe the police would give up on him. Maybe they would find out who killed Roberto and leave Mario alone. *Yeah, right. In your dreams*, he thought as he walked to his car.

Chapter 20

Greg Preston had been on the job for six months, and he still hadn't figured out just what was going on. Everything was so hush hush. There had not been one opportunity to check into the contents of any of the crates that he maneuvered every day. The other guys kept close eyes on his every move.

On several occasions, he had seen a sleek, black car drive up outside the warehouse near the office. But he never got a good view at the man who exited the vehicle. He only saw him from the back.

From what he had seen, however, he figured that somebody higher up was running this dog and pony show. Most regular guys would show up in a normal, everyday kind of car. Not one with a driver and blacked-out windows. Only dignitaries—or guys who didn't want to be seen—used those. He doubted that it was the former.

One monotonous Tuesday afternoon just after lunch, Greg happened to come around the corner of the warehouse at just the time another dark car pulled up. Ducking behind the wall, he peered around the building to get a better look. This time, a different guy got out. He was shorter and stockier than the previous occupant. As he walked to the office, he peered around nervously as if he was hoping not to have been seen by anyone. As the man walked up the steps to the office, Greg got a glimpse of his face. What was Mr. Franzoni doing here? Of course, he was the one who had sent Greg here in the first place. But why was he coming now? Where was the other guy?

Now was as good a time as any to find out what was really taking place in this dump. Making sure he'd be undetected, Greg quietly climbed the stairs to stand just outside the door, and leaned his ear against it.

"Where's Roberto?" asked Scrapper.

"Haven't you heard? He took a hit," replied Franzoni nervously.

"No, when?"

"Just a few days ago. The cops have already come calling, asking all kinds of questions," Mario replied.

"You didn't tell them anything, did you?" Scrapper bellowed.

Greg heard an anxious, "Of course not."

For a few moments, all was quiet. Then Scrapper asked, "So why are *you* here?"

With a little more bravado than he felt, Mario barked, "I've been given his territory. I'm checking on a problem with that last shipment."

Scrapper cleared his throat before answering. "What kind of problem?" It didn't sound to Greg like he wanted to know. With a much stronger voice, Mario stated, "One of the four crates never made it to its destination."

"What? That's not possible. I oversaw the shipment myself," yelled Greg's boss.

"Then you have a problem," stated the now more forceful Franzoni.

Scrapper asked, "What am I supposed to do about it? I saw it put on the truck. It was there when it left the warehouse. You'll have to check with the driver. Maybe he decided to take a cut for himself. Although I don't think he has any idea what's inside any of those crates. He's been driving for us a long time. I thought he could be trusted."

"Obviously not. It's up to you to find out. I think you know what will happen if it's decided you're at fault," warned Mario.

Greg heard footsteps coming toward the door and made a hasty retreat. He'd miss any more of the conversation, but wasn't about to stick around and get caught eavesdropping.

Entering the warehouse, he glanced up in time to see the car door slam and the vehicle heading out of the parking area.

I wonder what that was all about, he thought. Now, his curiosity was aroused even more. Whatever these crates held must be worth stealing. He speculated what had happened to Darius, the truck driver. He hadn't seen him in several days and was beginning to wonder if he had taken off with the merchandise. These jerks were not the kind of people you crossed, not if you valued your life.

Going back to his forklift, Greg contemplated finding out more, or getting another job. He certainly didn't want to spend more time behind bars, or worse yet, end up dead. He chewed on those thoughts the rest of the afternoon. No need to make a hasty decision. He'd have to think this one through.

★ ★ ★

A few days later, Todd looked up to see Kirk coming through the office door. "You wanted to see me?" he asked.

"Yeah, another body was found in a remote area on the south side of town."

Kirk sat in the chair opposite Todd's desk and questioned, "Any one we know?"

"No. He was Darius Morris, who has been driving for an import company for several years. Had a run in with the law a couple of years ago, but nothing major since," replied Todd.

"What else do we know about this guy?" asked Kirk.

"He was twenty-nine, single, kind of a loner. The boss at the company said he just did his job and didn't talk much to any of the other workers in the warehouse."

Kirk replied, "And let me take a wild guess, a bullet to the head, right?"

"Are you thinking what I'm thinking, that this has something to do with one Mr. Roberto Jenks? Ballistics is checking to see if the same gun was used. We'll know that in a little while."

Kirk was thoughtful before answering, "If it was the same gun, there's more to it than meets the eye. Why a big-time crook and a small-time truck driver? Who was really paying him? What kinds of things did he deliver? We have a lot of questions without answers."

"So far," reminded Todd.

"Yeah, so far. But I'm not about to sit around waiting for that report. What say we go have a talk with the owner of the import company? Then the customers of said company. You don't find worms for fishing without turning over a few rocks," smiled Kirk.

Chapter 21

A phone call had only confirmed that Darius had been a truck driver here, but other information had not been forthcoming. Wanting an on-site interview, the two detectives entered the office of the import company, and kept their eyes on the man behind the desk.

Showing their badges, Todd made the introductions, and then asked, "Are you the manager here?"

Sitting up a little straighter, Scrapper replied, "Yeah, owner, manager, jack-of-all trades. Harvey Chilton's the name. What can I do for ya?"

Already knowing the answer before he asked, Todd responded, "Did your company employ one Darius Morris as a driver?"

Looking a little uneasy, Mr. Chilton nodded.

"How long did he work here?"

"I don't know, maybe six or seven years. I think he came here right out of high school when junior college didn't quite fit him. Why?"

"Are you aware the Mr. Morris has been murdered?"

As if hoping to find some help from somewhere, Harvey nervously replied, "When he didn't show up for work, I figured something had happened to him. He is, or was, a pretty dependable fellow. Sorry to hear that."

Todd glanced at Kirk before asking, "Do you have any idea who might have had a beef with him? Or wanted to kill him? Who are his friends here?"

Chilton appeared in deep concentration on that before he answered, "Nah, I don't have a clue as to who would want to do him in. As to friends, he hardly spoke to anyone around here. Just did his job, and left at the end of the day. Never made trouble. Hardly knew he was around. Real antisocial, if you ask me. You can ask the other drivers, but I haven't any idea if he had any disagreements with any of the guys. If he did, I didn't hear about it."

Kirk replied, "Could you give us a list of all your employees, both past and present. Going back to when Darius started working here."

With a disgusted grimace on his face, the manager gave a grunt and agreed. "I'll take me a while to find all that kind of information. How soon do you want it?"

"As soon as possible," replied Todd. "The one responsible for his murder could very well be working right outside your door."

A startled expression told the detectives that Mr. Chilton did not like hearing those words.

"I'll have a list to you by the end of the day."

"Thank you. How many people do you employ now?"

Without hesitation, the manager replied, "We aren't a big organization."

Trying to hold in his frustration, Todd asked again, "And how many of them are working today?"

With a sigh, Mr. Chilton started to open up a bit and said, "There are six guys working today. There are ten on the roster, counting Darius. One guy is out sick; another is on vacation. The third one is on leave taking care of his sick mother. Of the rest, there are drivers and workers in the warehouse."

Before they could ask, he continued, "We do mostly short-term, in-state deliveries. Every so often there's a load that has to go out of state. We have all kinds of vehicles, from small cargo vans to a semi. I think Darius drove the big rig most of the time. Those were usually the long-distance jobs."

Kirk was writing down each piece of information as it was given.

Todd added, "And we will need a list of your customers, going back to when Darius began driving for you. Where you get the goods and to whom they are delivered. Also, the types of merchandise that gets transported."

Tensely, the manager replied, "That might take a bit longer. I don't have a secretary right now, and I'm not that savvy with a computer; but I'll do my best. I suppose you want that ASAP as well."

"We'd appreciate it," answered Todd. Then he added, "We'll start by questioning the workers who are in-house at the moment. Since you do short-range deliveries, they must come and go throughout the day. Is that right?"

"Yeah, I never know who's going to be here at any one time. I post a list of the deliveries that are scheduled to come in, and where they need to go. The drivers divvy up the routes. Gives them a little sense of ownership I guess. Plus, it's less work for me."

Not replying to that, Todd added, "Alright, thank you for your time. I'll expect those lists to me by the end of the day. My e-mail address is on the back of my card," he said as he handed the information to the agitated man.

Nodding in their direction, the manager asked if there was anything else he could do for them.

Declining, the two detectives left the office, determined to do their jobs and find the one who had killed what seemed to be an innocent man.

★ ★ ★

Questioning the two drivers who were in the warehouse, yielded little information. Neither of them knew Darius well at all. Neither could they come up with who might have wanted to do away with him. It seemed like a case of don't ask, don't tell. If they knew anything, they weren't spilling any beans.

They also questioned the other workers including the forklift operators. One of them was familiar to Todd but he couldn't quite place him at the moment.

Once in their car, Kirk said to Todd sarcastically, "That was sooo informative! Sometimes I wonder why people don't seem to care when one of their own is taken out so heartlessly."

Todd nodded in agreement. "According to them, none of them had even tried to make friends with Darius. That's just sad. Do your work, don't ask questions, and go home at night. Just to do the same thing all over again the next day. There had to be times when they weren't that busy for the guys to talk sports, or something. You'd think they would at least care a little about another human life."

After some thought, Kirk asked, "Could it be that they knew what Darius was doing, but were afraid to talk? I mean maybe they discovered he was cheating the company; but since their hands weren't clean either, they just kept the information to themselves."

"That's a definite possibility. Once we get those lists from Chilton, we can ask a lot more people a lot more questions. Right now, I'm stumped. If Darius was taking his share of the goods from the deliveries, why was it never discovered? Or was it, but someone was paid off to keep quiet?"

Many more scenarios were discussed as the two drove back to the precinct. Todd hated these kinds of cases where no one knew anything. Someone was always lying. And who was that guy he knew he recognized?

Chapter 22

Holding the phone in his sweaty hand, Scrapper waited for the other party to connect.

As soon as he heard the 'hello,' he blurted out, "The cops have been here asking questions about Darius. What am I going to do?"

"Settle down. What did you tell them?"

"Nothing! I tried to play it cool, like I hardly knew the guy. Didn't tell them anything, I swear."

There was a long pause before he heard, "Good. I hope you didn't act nervous. That's a dead giveaway if you did."

"How could I *not* be nervous? But I tried to play it cool. Gave them only what they already knew, that he drove the big rig for us, and I hadn't seen him in several days. That he was a loner, not mixing with the other guys much. What else was I supposed to say?"

"Okay, this is what we're going to do. Stick with your story, no embellishments. You do know what that means, right?"

"Yeah, I'm no dummy. But what if they come back again, or start nosing around some more? They talked with a couple of the other drivers and workers in the warehouse. They want a list of all the employees as well as all our customers. I put them off with telling them I'm not very tech savvy. But they want the lists by tonight." Panic was edging its way into Harvey's voice.

Mr. Big just sighed and then replied, "I will work up a safe list of customers and have it to you within the hour. You will give them only this list. Is that understood?"

"Yes."

"Yes?"

"Yes, sir."

"That's better. Go get yourself a stiff drink. It sounds like you could use one. I'll be in touch." With that, the phone line went dead.

Scrapper stood up from his desk and started pacing in the sparse office. Maybe he should just get out of town. Cut his losses and run. He didn't want to end up like Roberto or Darius. But if he knew these guys as well as he thought he did, they would find him and permanently silence him. Up to this point, he'd managed to slip under the radar, just doing his job and keeping his mouth shut. Taking a little here and a little there, without any notice. Now, he was in more hot water than a hard-boiled egg.

How was he ever going to get out of this predicament? He wasn't there when Darius was shot, but he knew what had happened to the extra crate. If the big man ever found out that he was behind its loss, he'd never be heard from again.

Right now, money seemed the furthest thing from his mind. Selling the contents of that crate had netted him several thousand dollars, but what was that when your life was at stake? Why hadn't he thought of that before now?

Could he be pegged for the murder? He remembered what Mario had said about why Roberto was eliminated. He had thought to outsmart the big guy. See how that worked out! Now he really was scared. Running seemed like the only alternative open to him. As soon as he got that list of suppliers and customers off to the police, he was going to do a vanishing act. He heard that Florida was nice this time of year.

★ ★ ★

After the cops had questioned him, Greg started doing his own soul searching. He recognized the one Detective but didn't give himself away. He'd rather not remember that the guy was the one who had arrested him and sent him to prison.

What kind of organization was this, anyway? People getting shot, merchandise missing, thugs in and out of the office. He had to find out what was going on. A plan began forming in the back of his mind as he signed out for the day.

Later that night, after he was sure everyone had gone home, he sneaked back to the warehouse. He'd fixed the side door so that he could get in without triggering the alarm. For some reason, there were no security cameras in or around the building. That had always made him wonder if the higher-ups thought they were immune to theft, or maybe they didn't want any evidence to incriminate them.

Dressed in all black and carrying a heavy-duty flashlight, he entered the huge area and saw the various-sized crates waiting for delivery. It was now or never. Moving into a far corner, he grabbed a crowbar from the counter and headed to one of the smaller crates.

With some muscle and effort, the top was off far enough for him to peek inside. Carefully moving the packing material aside, he spotted what he was trying to find. There were several carved statues. Laying the flashlight down so that it shone into the crate, he picked up two identical pieces. They weighed the same. Digging deeper, he grabbed a couple more. Just as he'd suspected, one was heavy and solid, while the other one felt much lighter.

Inspecting the bottom of the second one, he noticed a slight indention in the plaster. Pulling his pocket knife out, he dug away at the plug and out dropped a bag of white powder. Drugs! He should have known. Replacing the plug as best he could, he rewrapped the pieces, rearranged the packing material, and replaced the cover of the crate.

Quickly heading to the door, he checked to be sure that he'd left no evidence behind. Ducking into the darkness, he hurriedly walked away towards his rooming house.

Once safely inside his room, Greg finally drew a deep breath. Did he wipe his fingerprints off those statues? In his haste, he couldn't remember. Sweat broke out on his forehead as he tried to pull that piece of information into his consciousness. Pulling his handkerchief from his pocket to wipe his face when he remembered that he had used it to wipe off everything he had touched. Whew!

Now what? Could he be charged as an accessory? Even when he didn't know what was going on? Or did he?

Here he was, in his late-thirties, with nothing to show for his life. His step-father had died. His mother, who used to bail him out of his mishaps, was now off spending her inheritance. He hadn't seen or heard from her in months.

Maybe he should take to heart what his step-sister, Joan Travis, had told him years ago. *'Stop thinking about yourself and grow up.'* He hoped he was older and wiser now. He didn't relish the idea of going back to prison. Or ending up dead.

A new plan began to come together in his mind.

Chapter 23

Several months had passed in the budding relationship between Randy Burnett and Gerry Smart. Some days, Randy had to pinch himself to believe that someone as delightful as Gerry would even give him the time of day. She was becoming much more than a friend. Was he in love with her? He wasn't sure yet; but if not, then he was certainly in extreme like that was leading to love.

He didn't have many friends to whom he could go to ask questions about romance. It seemed strange to ask his mom, Sally. Although he knew that she and his late father had been in love with each other, he just couldn't seem to bring up the questions to her. Knowing her, she would be ready to plan a wedding, if he so much as asked for some helpful advice. Maybe he was selling her short, but it still felt rather awkward, nonetheless.

Gerry had come to dinner on several occasions and seemed to fit right in with him and Sally. His mom had often commented on what a lovely young woman she was and that she really liked her. But she hadn't pushed her son. She knew he wanted to be sure of the Lord's will before going to the next level with this delightful young lady. But in her heart of hearts, Sally already knew that they were perfectly matched. Randy and Gerry enjoyed a delightful relationship that seemed to grow deeper every time they talked or were together.

He had moved into his own small, one-bedroom apartment a few weeks ago, and was enjoying the feeling of being a true adult. He loved his mom dearly, but at his age, he just couldn't live at home any longer. He wanted to prove to himself, if to no one else, that he could take care of himself.

His parole officer had told him that another month was all he needed to follow him. Officer Peters begrudgingly admitted that Randy was one of a kind. Although there was never an opportunity for Randy to share much with the man, at least he seemed pleased with Randy's progress. He knew he didn't deserve the reprieve from the law, but was grateful when Peters said that he would recommend suspension of his parole for good behavior. That was affirmation enough for him. He thanked God every day for favor with the gruff but fair man.

With the Lord helping him, he had settled in to work, school, dating, and everything else without a hitch. But there still was that nagging doubt about love.

One day, with head down and shoulders slumped while he was rolling out some cookie dough; Fred wandered into the prep area.

"How are you doing today, my boy?" asked the gentle giant. Fred gave the appearance of strength, but was really tender inside. He expected nothing less than Randy's best, and held him to that exacting level. He was tough, but fair. But he could also commiserate with him about his walk with God and the things where he felt he was still failing to meet God's commands.

Exhaling, Randy replied, "Okay, I guess."

"You guess? What's really bothering you? You're usually so upbeat these days that this gloomy-gus attitude isn't like you. 'Fess up. You can't keep it to yourself or you'll burst," carefully teased his boss.

Straightening himself to his full height, Randy turned around and blurted out, "I'm in love with Gerry!" Realizing what he'd just said, he exclaimed, "Wow! Where did that come from? I've been trying to figure it out, and when you asked, I just knew!"

Smiling, Fred said, "Well, it's about time you figured that out!"

"What do you mean?"

"I've known for weeks that you were bitten by the love bug, and have been praying for you," replied the kind man.

"You have? How come you knew and I didn't?" asked the confused young man.

Gathering his thoughts, Fred replied, "Well, how many batches of baked goods have we had to throw out because your head was somewhere else? Like that batch of biscuits that didn't rise, could it have been you forgot the yeast? Or the cake that landed on the floor instead of in the oven? Or the scones that were hard as a rock? Or...."

"Okay, okay, I get your point. I have been kinda distracted lately. Sorry about the spoiled baked goods. I'm not that careless, really I'm not."

Fred laughed again and said, "Don't worry about it. When I was in love the very first time, I got lost on my way home from work because my mind was on a certain redhead."

"You were in love? What happened?" Randy asked.

"Oh, yes, at twenty-six, I was head-over-heels in love with Maureen. She was the best thing that had come along in my entire life. I couldn't seem to get enough of her. We dated for only three months before I got up enough courage to ask her to marry me."

"You got married? I never knew that. Where is she? Why have you never mentioned her?"

A sadness crossed Fred's face, and sighing he replied, "Only two weeks before our wedding, she was killed in a multiple-car accident on the freeway. She wasn't at fault, but that didn't change the outcome."

"Oh Fred, I'm so sorry. That must have been devastating."

"It was. I thought I would die. I wanted to, even tried a couple of times. But I guess the Lord had other ideas. I don't know why she had to die. She was the sweetest, kindest person I have ever met. She truly lit up my life. Although I wasn't a believer back then, she was, and everything about her exuded peace. She often shared her faith with me, wanting me to know and love her Savior. I don't know why she was willing to marry me even when I hadn't yet surrendered, but maybe she saw something in me that I couldn't see. I still miss her, even after all these years."

Randy agreed, "I can't even imagine what my life would be like without Gerry in it. She makes me laugh, she challenges me in my faith, and we can talk about everything. Is this love? I'm still so confused," admitted the love-struck baker.

Smiling widely, Fred responded, "Let me give you a piece of advice that was given to me all those years ago. If you can't imagine your life without that special person, then don't let it happen. Do something permanent about it. Propose, already!"
He went on, "I've never regretted asking Maureen to marry me. Those weeks leading up to the wedding were some of the happiest memories I have of our time together. What I wouldn't give to have just a few short hours again to express to her what knowing and loving her did for me. She might never have known it, but she set me on a path toward my Savior. I was just slow in reaching that destination. That was my fault, not hers. It wasn't for lack of her trying or, I'm sure, praying for me. I'll never be able to thank her enough for pointing me in the right direction. One day, I plan to tell her just that."

"Wow, again. I can't believe it! I've been so caught up in my own life; I never thought about what you might have experienced or if you would even know how I was feeling. Did you ever marry, or have you been a loner since you lost your first love?"

"Actually, I did find another good woman to marry. We were together for about twenty years, when she, too, was taken by way of cancer. We didn't have any kids, and I've always regretted that.

"I think her death was what sent me 'over the edge' so to speak. I started doing some not-so-ethical things at the place where I was the head baker. By then, I really didn't care if I was found out. In fact, I kind of hoped I would be.

"The Lord and the law finally caught up with me. It was a chaplain who came to the prison each week who led me into the fullness of salvation. I thank God every day for the dedication of that man. My wife and I had only attended church on occasion, so I have no idea where she's spending eternity. She was raised in church, so there's a possibility that she made it to heaven, but I won't know for sure until I get there. I sure hope I see her. It would be tragic to think she didn't make it," Fred said sadly.

At this admission, Randy grabbed Fred in a tight hug. Though neither of them was all that great at expressing their feelings, yet it felt good to offer whatever comfort he could to his friend and employer. When they broke the embrace, both of them were a little embarrassed.

Wiping his eyes with the corner of his apron, Fred choked out, "Thanks. I didn't even know I needed that! I've never shared much with anyone about Maureen. Loving her is a great memory, but not something I wanted to revisit because of the pain her death caused. Although the Lord has softened the hurt and loss, I still think about her and wonder what my life would have been like if we had married and had a family."

Blowing his nose in his handkerchief, he added, "But then, I never would have had to leave that great job, buy this place, and meet you! It's worth it to me to see how you've taken to this business and the talent you have for creating that exceeds my own. Remember, one day in the distant future, say four or five years, this will all be yours."

"Yeah, you keep reminding me of that! My classes are more than half over at the college. I'm learning so much. I never imagined how much it took to not only run a business but also 'do' the business, so to speak. There's so much more to it than making bread! How did you manage all that time before I came on the scene?"

"I can tell you, it wasn't easy. At first, when the business was small, I just opened for half a day and worked on the books at night. But soon, word got out that I was a decent baker, and I had to extend the daily hours from four to eight. I did hire a bookkeeper to help manage the business end of things; but he was only here a couple of years before he got a better-paying job. Can't say that I was getting much sleep before you showed up!"

As Randy contemplated all the changes in his life: an apartment, school, Gerry, the bakery, he realized that God was helping him handle it all. Well, except for the failed baked goods recently.

Fred has given me much to think about today. I'm so glad he took a chance on me in the first place. This is like home for me, coming here, creating sumptuous food, learning how to run a business. I appreciate the confidence he's placed in me, and want to do everything I can to live up to it.

He finally replied, "I will try to do a better job of keeping my mind on my work!"

Fred laughed out loud. "Just go ask that girl to marry you already. If you need any more push in that direction, let me know. I can see love on your face every time her name is mentioned. I don't think there's any possibility that she will turn you down. The few times that she's been in here to see you, the look on her face spells love with a capital 'L', just in case you were wondering."

"Really, you think she loves me too?" asked an anxious Randy.

"Oh, for heaven's sake. Go ask her. You'll never know unless you ask." Fred said this as he pushed Randy toward the front door.

"Now? You want me to go ask her now? But she's teaching her class right now. I can't just go in there and interrupt her."

"Why not? Do you have a ring yet?"

At Randy's questioning countenance, he added, "Well, what's keeping you? Go buy a ring, get the biggest bouquet of roses, or whatever is her favorite flower, and get busy. There's no time like the present!"

With excitement playing over his face, Randy took off his apron and threw it towards the hook on the wall. "Okay! I will!"

And with that, he was out the door and heading to the next phase of his life.

Chapter 24

The children were moving back to their seats from the blackboard, when there was a light knock at the door. To Gerry's surprise, Randy poked his head in and caught her attention. Smiling, she motioned him in with her hand.

As she followed him with her eyes, he seemed a bit nervous and shy. *What could he want, and why is he acting like that?*

When she came to meet him at the front of the classroom, he handed her the huge bouquet of flowers he had been hiding behind his back. Then, before she could manage a 'thank you,' he slipped to one knee. The children all got up from their chairs to see what was happening. Some of the girls began to squeal. She silenced them with a look.

When she realized what was taking place, Gerry covered her mouth with her hand.

"Gerry, you are the light of my life. I don't even want to think what my life would be like without you in it. I love you with all my heart. Will you please marry me?" Randy asked as he opened a small box to show her the ring he had just purchased only an hour before.

Gasping, she extended her left hand, and said a breathless, "Yes."

Placing the ring on her finger, Randy rose and took her in an embrace, kissing her chastely. "Thank you," he whispered in her ear following the kiss. "You've made me the happiest man on earth."

By this time the classroom had erupted in shouts, stomping, clapping, even some tears. The principle of the school had come to find out what the commotion was all about. One of the girls shouted, "He just asked Ms. Smart to marry him. Isn't it romantic?"

The man just stood there and shook his head in wonder. He thought, *well it's about time. Maybe now she can get her mind back on her job!*

He had noticed that Ms. Smart was somewhat distracted lately. She forgot her class on the playground; she left them in the gym after an assembly; and had a couple of parents questioning when she signed notes home with 'love, Gerry.'

Gerry quickly regained her composure and told the children to quiet down and take their seats. She walked with Randy to the door, promising to call him as soon as school was over for the day. The principle had smiled at the couple as he retreated out of the classroom. That was the kind of noise that deserved to be allowed. It wasn't every day that one of his teachers got a marriage proposal. Ms. Smart was a great teacher, and he hoped he wouldn't be losing her anytime soon.

Once Randy had departed, Gerry tried to get her mind back on the task at hand. She kept admiring the lovely solitaire on her ring finger, and had to drag her attention away from what had just taken place.

The children had taken their seats but were still whispering about the class disruption. The girls had dreamy expressions on their faces; the boys were less thrilled but still glad to have the distraction from doing school work.

Finally, Gerry let out a deep breath, and said to the children, "Well. That certainly wasn't in my lesson plans!"

Everyone broke out into wonderful laughter. She loved these children as if they were each one of her own. Each new class brought its trials, but it also brought new lives to change and challenge.

Soon, hands went up all over the room as one child after the other asked questions about her relationship with Randy: who was he; how had they met; when would they get married; and could they come to the wedding.

Seeing the time on the clock, Gerry decided that trying to finish with writing lessons today was a lost cause. There were only a few minutes left in the day, so she answered each question as honestly as she thought these children could manage.

All the while, her mind was on the handsome man to whom she had responded with the most important answer of her life. Did she love Randy? Absolutely! She couldn't imagine her life without him either. He filled something in her she didn't even know she was missing. Coming to Jesus had settled her heart and given her peace. But the love she felt for Randy was almost like icing on the cake. She laughed at her comparison.

When the final bell rang, the children had already gone through the daily routine for the end of the day, clearing their desks, and putting their things in their backpacks or bags. At Gerry's nod, they somewhat quietly ran to the door and were headed out to the buses or walkways, none too quietly. She was sure the monitors would have fun trying to control her bunch this day. But for some reason, she just didn't care. Accepting Jesus had been the best day of her life. But this had been the next best day ever! How could one person contain such happiness?

★ ★ ★

As Gerry walked out of the school toward the parking lot, she felt as if she was floating. Whatever convinced calm, gentle Randy to propose so dramatically? She had dreamed of this day, but had never expected it to happen as it did. Actually, she was really pleased that he did it in front of her students. They were her 'family' here and she was delighted to include them in the event.

Once she reached her car, she took out her phone and punched in Randy's number. He answered on the first ring, "Hi Miss almost-wife Smart."

She burst out laughing. "Hi to you, Mr. almost-husband Burnett."

The joy in their voices could not be contained. "Meet me at the park, across from my apartment?" Randy asked. "We have a lot to talk about."

"Yes, sir," she answered with another laugh.

★ ★ ★

Soon, she was parking her car and heading to their favorite bench overlooking the small pond in the center of the park. She didn't even have to ask where in the park they would meet. Many times they had spent hours talking in the secluded spot. It became 'theirs' not long after they started dating.

There had been concerts, movies, dinners out, plus those endless walks in the park. They had visited each other's churches, gone on picnics, watched softball games, and generally spent as much time together as their individual busy schedules would allow. Had that only started six months ago?

Spotting Randy before he saw her, she stopped to take in the outline of his handsome face. Waiting for the man that God had intended for her had taken some perseverance on her part. She had almost thought that God had forgotten her prayers for a husband. Gazing at Randy, she thanked God that she had not gotten ahead of Him by settling for second-best.

Randy turned just then and beamed at her as he watched her walk down the trail to his side. Once she reached him, he took her in his arms and just held her. There was such comfort and peace that surrounded them. They could have stood there forever, just knowing the mutual love that was between them.

Reluctantly, Randy let her go, but took her hand as he led her to the bench. "Were you surprised? Was that okay? Did I embarrass you?"

Smiling, Gerry reached over and planted a firm kiss on her intended's check. "You couldn't have done any better! Yes, I was surprised! I had no idea that you were even thinking about love or marriage. I hoped you were, but we never really talked about it. And, no, I was not the least bit embarrassed. My class was beside themselves with happiness for me. Did you notice that the principle came into the classroom, found out what was taking place, and left without so much as a comment? He did have a smile on his face though."

Randy relaxed for the first time in nearly an hour. "I'm so glad you said yes! I was so scared you'd refuse and we'd both be humiliated."

"Why did you ever think I'd say 'no' to you?"

Slowly letting out a breath, Randy replied, "Well, I could hardly believe that God had brought you into my life, and I didn't want to mess that up."

"May I ask, why today?"

"You aren't going to believe this," he replied as he went on to tell her about his conversation with Fred.

"Oh, God bless that man. I knew I liked him!" was Gerry's response. "I was beginning to wonder exactly how you felt. I think I started to love you that first day at the bakery when you were so interested in my plans for the students. You weren't put off by a woman who knew what she wanted to do and wasn't afraid to do it. That can be intimidating to some men."

"Are you kidding? I think that's when I started to love you, although I was a bit slow in recognizing it! You were so confident and sure that you had a good plan and wanted to see it through, no matter what it took. I admired that. You saw a need and wanted to fill it. That takes strength, but it also speaks of character."

As they went on to discuss other times through their days of dating and getting to know each other, it didn't take long for them to realize that something, or Someone, else was directing their footsteps. Gerry didn't judge Randy for his past life. He didn't judge her for her take-charge attitude when it came to her students. Together, they marveled over how their lives had intertwined even before they met. She had prayed for him in her Sunday school class, never imagining that she would one day meet him, let alone fall in love with him. And he had been mindful of those prayers from people he had never met, but who cared for his lost soul. The love of God is truly something wonderful!

Chapter 25

Jenny Chambers felt like she was in a whirlwind. Ever since the reading of Aunt Harriet's will, she could think of nothing else. *All that money! And what were they going to do with that big house? Do we move in, or do we sell it? Where do we start? Why had Aunt Harriet been so generous to us?* She had a lot more questions than answers.

Todd and Jenny decided not to make any quick decisions about the inheritance. They had been told one should take some time making big decisions after a major life-changing experience. And this was major!

A week or two later, Jenny felt like she could voice her thoughts wisely, so when Todd got home from work that evening and the kids were safely in bed, Jenny began asking him some of the things that had been swirling around in her head.

"Honey, what are we going to do? That house is so big and needs a lot of work. Do you think it would be a good place for us to live? It's in a well-established neighborhood. And it's not that far from Timmy's school."

Todd sighed. Switching gears from solving murders to talking about houses was harder than it should be. Gathering his thoughts, he replied, "Well, we do need more space. Ever since Abby was born, it seems like this place has shrunk. And we have talked about finding a larger house. I know that repairs, and maybe some remodeling, would have to be done on that big old house, but maybe that's the answer to our needs."

Jenny smiled for the first time all day. "You know what? I think you just read my mind. I've always loved that house. So many rooms to explore, especially the attic. I'd hate to sell it out of our family. It's been a part of my life for as long as I can remember."

Continuing, she added, "I have to admit that I've been wrestling with this for days. But it seems like such an easy solution. We could use some of the money to fix it up just the way we want it. There's plenty of room for everyone to have their own space. You could have an office of your own instead of working out of our dining room! I could even have a sewing and craft room that would be off-limits to the kids. I could shut the door and not have to put everything away every time I had to stop in the middle of a project."

Getting excited at the prospect, Todd added, "Yeah. We could modernize the kitchen and bathrooms. Probably have to fix the roof and then maybe add a sun room to the back. The yard needs some tender loving care since Harriet wasn't able to work in the flowerbeds for the last few years. I know she had a gardener, but he didn't have her eye for color and style. With that big back yard we could put in a swing set for the kids, maybe even a swimming pool?"

Joining in his excitement, Jenny continued, "Oh, and paint all the rooms bright colors, and maybe get some new furniture. Although several of the pieces are probably antiques, I would like to add my own tastes in furnishings. Is there room to expand the garage to fit two cars? Maybe make a breezeway or something to connect it to the house? I don't like getting out of the car and walking through the rain to the house!"

At this, Todd chuckled and remarked, "My little princess!"

"Oh, you," Jenny laughed as she punched him lightly on the arm.

Finally, she said with a sigh, "Why did I get so worked up over this? All I had to do was wait until we could talk about it. Somehow, I knew you would have the right perspective. I'm sorry if I've been distracted lately, and haven't shared my thoughts with you."

Taking her in his arms, Todd leaned down and placed his chin on her head. "Sorry I've been so distracted with the cases that I'm working on that I didn't see you were distressed. Guess we both needed to step back and get some clearer insight as to what we should do. How about if we pray about it? I know God has all the answers."

Together, they bowed their heads and took the matter to the great Administrator. When they finished, the heavy burdens lifted, and they were confident that they would do what was best for their little family.

Todd then added some more ideas, "We need to see about finding a good money manager to help with the investments and long-term planning for the remaining funds. You know, like college funds for the kids, our retirement, travel, that kind of thing."

Jenny nodded her agreement. "I'm sure Mr. Thornton could give us some names to help on that score. Right now, I think he's handling everything, but that's not his area of expertise. Did he mention if Aunt Harriet had a stock broker, or money manager?"

Thinking about her question, Todd replied, "I don't remember if he did, but I'm sure there has to be someone that Aunt Harriet trusted in that area. Why don't you call his office tomorrow and find out. We might as well go with someone who is already familiar with those investments and any other plans that Aunt Harriet had set in motion. It's possible there's more that we don't even know about."

Then he added, "I'll check with the guys at work to see if any of them can recommend a good contractor who can give us an estimate on what we want to do. Once we decide what that is, of course!"

Todd finally took a breath saying, "Hey, we just practically planned our next five years. Let's step back and take some time to think through all these steps. We could talk to our folks and get some insight from them. They were young and full of ideas once. Maybe we aren't seeing the whole picture."

"Okay," agreed Jenny. "I'll call my mom tomorrow and set up a lunch date with her and Tony to tell them some of our ideas. How about you talk to your parents soon too? I want to make sure we do this right. It's too big of a windfall to just jump into it. Even if we feel good about it right now, God will keep us on the right path if we don't run ahead of Him."

Todd agreed, and then said with a smirk, "Now that that's decided, can I read my newspaper?"

Laughing, Jenny gave him a kiss on the forehead and went to put away the laundry she had done earlier in the day.

Chapter 26

Life had gotten very busy for Randy as he finished up his schooling, worked a full forty-hour week at the bakery, and made plans to be married in less than three months.

Randy and his mom were in his kitchen eating an early dinner that he had prepared. "When did things start moving so fast? It seems as though it was only a few weeks ago when I got out of prison and started my new position as an assistant baker. Now I'm making plans for the future with the love of my life. When God moves, He moves quickly," Randy said between bites of his beef stew.

"I know," Sally exclaimed. "I'm so excited about your upcoming wedding that I'm nearly beside myself. I've never had a child get married before!" Her face was wreathed in smiles and her eyes were glistening.

Randy took a swallow of his water before adding, "Well, I've never gotten married before either! I'm so glad that Gerry and her family are handling most of the details for the ceremony. I just have to figure out where we're going on our honeymoon, and try to keep my mind on my tasks at work. I'll be so glad when this last class is over so that will be one less thing to occupy my mind."

"How are your classes? Have you learned a lot? It was so generous of Fred to pay your way to school. He's a real sweetheart," Sally added.

Randy leaned back in his chair while trying to pull his thoughts together. "You know, Mom, I never thought that God would be so good to me considering all the rotten things I did. My job at the bakery has given me the confidence I was lacking. Fred is a great teacher, patient and thorough. I don't know where I'd be if he hadn't hired me."

"Just another answer to many prayers, isn't it?"

"That's for sure. Then, to meet and fall in love with Gerry has been more than I could have imagined."

Sally commented, "That's what it says in the Word about God being able to do exceedingly above what we can ask or think."

"He sure did for me. In answer to all your prayers and those of your friends, not only did He save me just before I was arrested, but He also was with me through all those years in prison. Then He sent me to just the right job; and on top of that, He sent Gerry into our bakery for her sweets. She could have gone anywhere; but instead, she walked into my life like a bright ray of sunshine!" Randy reminisced.

"Boy, you are waxing poetic these days! It must be love," teased his mother.

Lowering his head so as not to let Sally see his smile, Randy just laughed under his breath. Every thought of Gerry made him smile. She was perfect! Her passion, her faith, her smile, her quiet manner, all added up to perfect in his estimation.

As if reading his thoughts, Sally added, "Just remember one thing. Neither one of you is perfect, but together you make up a whole that can strive to please God and His perfection. When the Word tells us to be perfect it actually means to be mature. As I've watched you grow in your faith and your responsibilities, I'd say you are well on your way."

"Thanks, Mom. You always know what to say to keep me grounded. I know that I'm not perfect, so I don't want to put Gerry on a pedestal of perfection either. We are just two people whom

God brought together to become one. I give you permission to let me know when I get out of balance in that equation."

"Oh, no. That's not my job! I'll leave that to our Heavenly Father. He's much better at pointing out and correcting our flaws. And believe me, your new spouse will see them as well. She will even exhibit a few of her own. That's why you both must depend on the Lord for your direction and help. Love may conquer all, except who takes out the garbage or how to load the dishwasher!" Sally replied with a wide grin.

"Gotcha!" laughed Randy as he took his dirty dishes to the sink.

Randy had been in his own apartment for three months now, he enjoyed fixing dinner for Sally at least once a week. After all the meals she had made for him, it was the least he could do. She had taught him many of her recipes for those delicious meals and had painstakingly directed him through his own attempts. At least neither he nor Gerry would starve!

Just thinking about her brought another smile to his face. How could he be so lucky? No, blessed was the word. And to know that she had been praying for him all these years before they met was beyond his comprehension—that God loved him so much.

★ ★ ★

As Randy reached for his diploma from the junior college President, he beamed from ear to ear. He'd done it! He'd finished his courses, plus a couple of others that he'd added along the way. Now he had his certificate and could move forward doing whatever God had in store for him. Since he wasn't even sure what that would be except for working at the bakery, he knew that all things were working together for his good.

Once the short ceremony was completed, Randy met Sally in the lobby. Grabbing her up in a hug he twirled her around before placing her feet back on the floor. "I did it!"

"There was never any doubt. You were driven to complete everything. And to think, you made the Dean's list at that! I am so proud of you!"

Just then, Gerry and her family came up to him. Taking her in his arms he squeezed her tight and gazed into her eyes with such longing that everyone had to turn away from the scene. Catching his breath, he gave her a quick kiss and then thanked her family for attending the awards ceremony.

"We're proud of you, Son," her dad, John, said. Already they had welcomed him into the family, even though the wedding was still two weeks away.

Walking arm-in-arm out of the auditorium, Randy guided Gerry to the newer car he had been able to purchase. They were all meeting at a restaurant to celebrate this milestone in Randy's life.

Soon, seated around a large table with their drinks and food ordered, Gerry's father turned to Randy and asked, "So, now what, young man? Will you go on to more schooling or what? How do you plan to support my daughter?" he said with a smile on his face. They had had this discussion before so Randy wasn't blind-sided by the question.

"I've been giving it a lot of thought and prayer," he said as he looked over at Fred on the other side of the table. Fred nodded his head so Randy continued, "I think I'll be learning all there is to running a bakery. Fred has generously offered me a partnership in his business with the understanding that one day I will buy him out."

Everyone turned to Fred and clapped for his benefit. He in turn smiled widely while the red creeped up his neck to his cheeks. He was not a man who liked to be the center of attention, but he loved Randy like the son he never had. Fred was delighted that Randy had taken him up on his offer.

Gerry added, "After we're married, we'll be living in my house which is actually closer to the bakery than Randy's apartment. I'm so proud of him and what he's accomplished."

Most of this was not new information to those present, but it solidified the immediate future for the young couple. Only God knew what was to come after that.

Chapter 27

Jenny finished taping the last box as she and Todd prepared to move into the remodeled house her beloved aunt Harriet had left to her.

For a couple of months after receiving her inheritance from Aunt Harriet, Jenny and Todd had been learning so much about what God planned for them. They had talked to a dozen different people about their desires concerning the house Harriet had left them, and all the financial income. Finally, they decided to make the move.

There was six months of picking out contractors, cabinets, flooring, paint, furniture and fixtures. Plus sorting and disposing of closets and drawers full of memories that were special to the dear woman but were of no value to them.

Then there was the chore of getting their home ready for sale, and keeping it clean and picked up at the same time. They had known this day would come, but it still was bitter sweet to have to leave their first home as man and wife. This was their children's first home. But the move felt right, and the young couple who purchased their house reminded Jenny of the two of them those few short years ago.

Now she and her family would be moving into the large house with their meager belongings. She was sure that they would be engulfed in the space, going from a three-bedroom townhouse to a six-bedroom mansion. At least that was how she viewed the century-old home.

Todd came up behind Jenny and wrapped his arms around her. "All done? Are you ready for this new chapter in our lives?"

Leaning back into his strong arms, Jenny replied, "As ready as I'll ever be. I can't believe that we are actually leaving this place. Although I knew this day would arrive since we were beginning to burst the seams, I just hate that it had to be due to the passing of Harriet. I still miss her so much."

Turning her around to face him, Todd said, "I do too. But I'm sure she would be pleased with all the improvements that we've made to the house. No doubt we will feel her presence in every room as we think about all that she meant to us. It is at least one way to keep her with us."

Sighing, Jenny just nodded her head. No time for tears or sentimentality. The movers were pulling up out front and it was time to go. Because of Harriet's generosity, they were able to hire a moving company to do all the hard work instead of having to depend on friends with strong backs!

She and Todd had done much of the packing themselves, moving special items to the house little by little. Mostly, it was the furniture and heavy boxes left for the movers.

Within short order, the truck outside was filled with most of their earthly possessions. After offering the hard-working men some cold water bottles left for just that purpose, it was time to follow them to their new address.

★ ★ ★

Two days later, Jenny sat at the kitchen table with her mom, Kathleen, as they took time for a breather. Kathleen had been a big help in emptying the boxes for the kitchen and the four bathrooms, deciding with Jenny where everything would go, and then remembering where that was!

Having so much room actually gave everyone some breathing space. Timmy and Abby each had their own room, plus they had another bedroom for all their toys.

Todd had an office to call his own. And Jenny now had her craft and sewing room that was all for her. They had the attic remodeled into a spacious master bedroom and bathroom. She could just hear Harriet's laugh as she saw the life and joy that had come to her house. Jenny couldn't help smiling at the thought.

"What's making you smile like that?" asked Kathleen as she sipped her tea.

"I was just thinking about how happy Aunt Harriet would be to see us enjoying this wonderful house. It had to have been lonely and quiet for her rattling around in all this space. It's as if a tornado was let loose with all the work that was done, and the kids having more than a few feet of room to move. It's certainly not going to be quiet or lonely for us. We feel so blessed that I'm often lost for words," Jenny replied, wiping a tear from her eye with her napkin.

Admiring the newly remodeled kitchen, Kathleen offered, "You've done a wonderful job of planning and making this room so functional. I love the center island and the amount of counter space you've added. Taking out the wall between the kitchen and dining room makes it so open and light. It's modern but still fits the total décor of the house's design. I'm so proud of you," she finished, dabbing at her eyes.

"Thanks, Mom that means a lot to me. You don't think we've done too much? I mean, Aunt Harriet did some updating along the way, but it was far from practical. She probably didn't watch as many home-improvement shows on TV as I do! That's where I got so many ideas as to what I wanted and what would work.

"And the contractor we hired actually listened to me and worked his magic. It's everything I envisioned. How can one person get so blessed with such material things as granite counters and tile flooring?" laughed Jenny.

"Don't sell yourself short. You worked hard to get what you wanted. It was Harriet's generosity that made it possible. I'm sure she knew she could trust you with her home—and her finances. That's why she left them to you."

"Well, I know she's enjoying her 'mansion' in glory far more than we are the one she left to us. I'm just grateful that one day we will be reunited and I can thank her in person for all she did for us. Not just the material things, but the rich spiritual heritage she left us. That's what will last for eternity. There's no way to know until then the impact she made on so many lives, including mine."

"Yes, she was one remarkable woman, used by God in ways I'm sure even she didn't know."

They went on to talk about some of the lessons that they had learned from the dear lady. She had been not only spiritual but also practical as well. Jenny hoped that she could have even a small impact on others that would mirror her dear aunt.

Finishing up their tea and conversation, Kathleen asked if there was anything more that she could do to help Jenny in getting settled.

"I guess we can tackle my craft room. Those boxes are not going to unpack themselves!"

"Sounds like a plan to me. Let's go," offered a rested and eager Kathleen. Known for her sense of organization, she knew that the two of them could do wonders in setting up everything to Jenny's approval. This was actually fun! Tiring, but satisfying nonetheless.

Chapter 28

Twice more, Greg Preston had discovered the true contents of the shipments that went through the warehouse. There had been more drugs in one, and diamonds in another.

He was now faced with what to do with the information--and how soon he should try to find another job. He didn't want to be implicated in any of the goings on here if the cops decided to dig deeper into the death of Darius. Even though he'd not known what was going on in the past, if he was taken in for questioning, he would have to tell what he knew and when he knew it. Waiting too long would seem as though he'd approved of the activities.

One evening as he thought through all that he had done in his life, he began to finally admit to himself that he'd made a lot of mistakes. For one, always getting in trouble with the law and having his Mom and step-Dad, Hank Pendleton, bail him out wasn't the most adult thing he could have done. Here he was, well into his thirties, with nothing to show for his life except a prison record, several trips to drug rehab, and a secret as big as the Titanic.

Maybe his step-sister Joan Travis had been right all along. He needed something or someone to help him make something of himself. He certainly didn't want the rest of his life to be the same as the past.

The more he thought about her words to him, her 'preaching' to him, the more he wondered if she actually knew what she was talking about. Could there be a higher figure at work that actually cared about him and wanted something better for his life? Would he help him in his current dilemma?

Making up his mind to find out, Greg called Joan and asked if he could come see her. He was surprised when she agreed. He wouldn't tell her what he knew, but he hoped that she wouldn't judge him for his past. She'd always treated him kindly, even when she blew up at him on her visit when he was in prison. She later apologized for losing her temper, but he hadn't been willing to listen then. Maybe now he should.

★ ★ ★

On Saturday afternoon, Greg knocked on her apartment door with trembling hands. When had she ever made him afraid? What was he afraid of now? Would she welcome him with open arms or with disdain?

Before he could think of any more questions, the door opened and Joan reached out to him with a big hug. So much for not being welcomed.

"Greg, it's so good to see you. How have you been? Come on in, please, and made yourself at home," Joan said in a rush. She had been stunned when he had called and asked to meet with her. Only God knew what he wanted and what she would say to him.

"Thanks," Greg mumbled as he took a seat on the side chair by the sofa. There were cups and a coffee carafe on the table in front of him, with some baked goodies on a small plate.

"Please help yourself to a cup of coffee and something to eat. It's not much, but I hope you like it," Joan said with a little bit of trepidation. Seating herself on the sofa, she took a deep breath, easing it out as she reached to pour the coffee.

After a few attempts at conversation with meaningless pleasantries, Joan finally took the lead. "So, Greg, is there something in particular that you wanted to talk about today?"

Joan had been praying for Greg for so many years that she was beginning to wonder if God would ever answer. Could today be the day? No sense in getting ahead of herself, she thought as Greg sat up a little straighter in his chair.

"Yeah, you could say that. I've been doing a lot of thinking about my life, or lack thereof. Can't say I'm too proud of the things I've done. None of it has gotten me very far. To tell you the truth, I'm tired of running."

Joan took a swallow of her coffee and relaxed for the first time since he walked in. Turning the whole conversation over to the great Orchestrator, she just nodded for him to continue.

"I used to think I had the world by the tail. I could do whatever I wanted and not have to pay the price for my actions. Mom usually bailed me out so I didn't have to suffer any consequences or at least nothing that had any lasting effect on me.

"Drug rehab only lasted for a short time, and I was right back where I started. Couldn't seem to rid myself of that straightjacket.

"Then I got caught in that phone scam. Mom wasn't any help at all. She thought I should learn from my mistakes this time. Too many years of my life were paid back for that stupid idea." Greg took a long drink from his cup and reached for a brownie. Taking a bite, he put the rest down on his napkin and continued.

"I've been clean ever since I got out of the joint. Got a job working in a warehouse moving crates around with a forklift. Not very challenging, but it's a paycheck. My accommodations are more or less adequate, but certainly not where I had envisioned my life by now.

"What I'm trying to say, I guess, is I want more out of my life. You've told me about this Jesus for years but I haven't wanted to listen. I didn't think I needed anyone, even though I used Mom and your Dad all the time. When even they couldn't or wouldn't help, I began to wonder if maybe I'd been wrong, or shortsighted." He stopped, a bit embarrassed by his admission.

He whispered, hopefully, "Do you think He could be interested in someone like me?"

Joan smiled at his honesty, and with all the love in her heart that she could find, she began to tell him about the Best Friend and Helper he would ever meet, showing him specific passages and verses in the Word to back up what she was saying.

He had lots of questions for which God gave her answers every time.

After a half hour of back and forth, Greg bowed his head and said the most important words of his life. He invited the Lover of his soul to come in, forgive his sins, clean out the rubble, and make him new.

When he glanced back up at Joan, his face was alight with an inner glow that made her heart rejoice for the transformation she saw right before her eyes.

"Wow! He's really real! I feel like a hundred-pound weight has been taken off my shoulders." Facing the window, he commented, "when did the sun shine so bright?'

Looking at Joan again, he exclaimed, "You're beautiful! How did I miss that all these years?" He got up and literally danced around the room. "I've never felt so light, so happy, or so free!"

Joan just sat back with tears of joy running down her face. She didn't even try to remove them. They represented the many hours of prayer she had said for this lost young man.

Finally, settling down a bit, Greg retook his chair, and said, "Now what? What can I do to keep this? I don't want to ever go back to who I was before. This is too good to not want to share it with the world!"

Joan laughed out loud, Greg joining her.

"Do you have a Bible?" she asked.

"Yeah, I think you gave me one a long time ago. I don't know where I put it though. Why?"

"It's now time to learn all you can about this new life you've gained," she replied. Going to a bookcase nearby, she pulled a New Testament off the shelf and handed it to Greg.

He took it reverently in his hands and flipped through the pages. Landing on one, he began to read. Soon he was lost in the words, ignoring his hostess.

Isn't God's love amazing? Thought Joan as she sent up her prayers of thanksgiving for Greg's salvation. It appeared she would be mentoring him for some time to come. But it was a joyful thought that added to the huge smile on her face.

Soon, Greg drew himself away from the life-giving Word and smiled at her. "I've got so much to learn," he said. "I just read that Jesus said I could have an abundant life. I want that! Not stuff, but peace and all that goes with it."

Joan replied, "The Word is alive, and the more you learn, the more you want to learn. I'll be glad to help you get started. Begin where you were, in the book of John. Write down any questions you have and together we can discover the answers. I don't want to just tell you. I want you to find out for yourself what it says and how it applies to your life."

Rising again to his feet, Greg came over to Joan and hugged her fiercely. "How can I ever thank you? I don't know why I didn't listen sooner, but I'm so glad you didn't give up on me."

Joan returned his hug and said, "I determined to keep praying until God answered. There's an acronym that says "PUSH"—pray until something happens! Even though my prayers for your salvation have finally happened, now I'll be praying for your growth in your faith."

Greg again smiled widely before he added, "With your help, and God's, I want to learn all I can."

After making plans to meet every other Saturday, Greg left with a little jaunt in his walk and a huge grin. He felt lighter than air!

After he left, Joan fell to her knees in gratitude to God for this answer to prayer. He had heard and He had answered. She didn't have words to express her thanks but knew He knew her heart. After several minutes she again sat on the couch and picked up her own Bible. Thumbing through it until she found just what she was hunting for, she read softly from I John 4:14-15: *"Now this is the confidence that we have in Him, that if we ask anything according to His will, he hears us. And if we know that He hears us, whatever we ask, we know that we have the petitions that we have asked of Him."*

It may have taken longer than she wanted, but the answer did come because she knew that it was God's will for Greg to know his Savior. Nothing could contain her joy! Again thanking the Lord for the truth in those words, she sat back and laughed out loud.

Chapter 29

Following Greg's transformation, his time spent with Joan helped him in learning all he could about his new life. His coworkers had notice the change in his demeanor, but had not asked what it meant. Greg decided to learn more before he started witnessing to them. If they had questions he couldn't answer, he didn't want to disappoint them or God.

The large elephant in the room remained. What was he going to do with the information he had? Should he go to the police? Would they even believe him considering his past?

He'd been praying about it ever since he learned about taking his needs to the Lord. But he'd had no indication yet of what to do.

One Saturday at Joan's, he decided to be even more candid with her.

"Joan, I have a question. If someone knows something that will get a lot of people into trouble but doesn't say anything, is that like lying?"

Joan nodded carefully at her new student and then responded, "Would that someone be you?"

Twisting his hands, Greg replied, "Yeah. I know something about what's going on in the warehouse; but I'm afraid to go to the authorities 'cause they might not believe me that I'm not involved. What should I do?"

Not wanting to give a flip response, Joan thought for a few moments, asking the Lord to give her the right answer.

"I'm sure you've prayed about this, right?" she asked.

"Yeah, but I still don't know what to do. I think I should talk to someone, but if these guys find out it was me who ratted on them, my life could be in danger," he admitted.

Taking a shuddering breath, Joan was quiet for a few more moments. "Would it help if you talked with a police detective I know, off the record? He's a committed Christian and I'm sure he would want to try to help you. I think you might remember him, Detective Todd Chambers. He's a good cop." Greg remembered. Todd had been the one to arrest him and Janetta when they tried that phone scam.

Thinking over her suggestion, Greg replied, "Yeah, I could do that. Maybe he could offer me some kind of protection or something."

Nodding and reaching for her phone, Joan dialed Jenny and Todd's number, hoping they were home.

"Hello, Joan," Todd said. "How nice to hear from you today. How are you?"

"I'm blessed beyond measure, and you?" she asked.

"I can agree with those sentiments entirely," he replied.

"Todd, I've got a problem I'm hoping you can help me untangle."

"Sure, what can I do for you?" Todd asked, his curiosity getting the better of him. Through the events that led to the arrest of a gentleman several years ago, he had met and learned to know and admire Joan and her walk of faith. He couldn't imagine what kind of problem she might be having. He prayed that he would be able to help.

"Someone dear to me has told me he has some information he needs to take to the authorities, but in so doing it might jeopardize his life. What should he do?" Joan hoped she hadn't been too vague.

When Todd didn't answer right away, she was almost ready to tell him to forget it. Todd answered her, "Would it be helpful if I talked with this person, informally, to see if what he has to say is worth investigating?"

With a sigh of relief, Joan said, "That would be wonderful. I hate to ask further, but are you free right now? We could come to you or if you'd rather, you could come here. I know it's an imposition, but it's really important."

She could hear Todd saying something to Jenny, and then he came back on the phone. "I can be at your place in a half hour. Will that work?"

"Oh yes, thank you. I do appreciate your taking your time from your family for this. Please tell Jenny thanks for sharing you today."

"I'll do that. See you in a few." Todd ended the call.

Turning to Greg, Joan informed him, "It's all set. Detective Chambers will be here in about half an hour." She went on to tell Greg how she had met Jenny, and then Todd during the ordeal with the stolen pin and all the other items.

Greg marveled at how God was already working on his behalf. He just hoped he'd have the courage to tell this guy all that he knew. He didn't want to get in any trouble, and he certainly didn't want to end up a statistic.

★ ★ ★

Todd arrived right on time. After introductions, and recognizing Joan's step-brother Greg, he said, "We've prayed for you for years, young man. So glad to know you are now a part of the real family," replied Todd.

He put Greg at ease with that statement. Greg was in awe that people he'd never met had been praying for him. Maybe this guy could help him after all, even though he had been the one to arrest him years ago. But that was in the past, right?

"Why don't we sit down while I get us some more coffee? You two get acquainted, I'll be right back," Joan said as she headed for the kitchen. She was doing a lot of praying for those two as she set about making coffee and putting everything on a tray to take to the living room.

"Why don't you tell me more about yourself?" Todd said to Greg.

"Well, you probably know more than I want to admit," Greg said rather sheepishly.

"Not really, but I'd like to hear your take on things," offered Todd with a smile.

Soon Greg was talking about his life and his many mistakes, culminating with his redemption right here not that many weeks ago.

Todd nodded in all the right places as he heard the familiar tale. Since he had been the one to arrest Greg and Janetta, he didn't want to seem biased about all that was being revealed.

Finally, Greg stopped his tale just short of the information that was burning a hole in his gut. He had to get this out or it was going to overwhelm him.

Joan returned with the coffee and some cookies. "I'll just leave you two to talk. I'm sure if it's anything serious, Todd will be able to sort it out."

"Please stay," Greg said, "I don't want any secrets between us."

Surprised but pleased, Joan nodded and took a seat.

Taking a big breath, Greg began, "As I said, I've been working at this warehouse since I got out of prison. It's an okay job as jobs go, but then my curiosity began to get the better of me." He told about the car with the dark windows, the death of one of the drivers, the secrecy that seemed to be everywhere, and then his discovery of the 'merchandise' that was hidden in the crates.

Todd had been taking a few notes but sat up when Greg told about the drugs and diamonds.

He began asking more pertinent questions, details that told Greg there was more to the story than even he knew.

Finally, exhausted with the telling, Greg sat back and asked, "Now what do I do? If they know that I told the police about this, I could just disappear. I don't want a bullet in the back of the head. Can you help me?" was his desperate plea.

Nodding, Todd replied, "You don't know how much I appreciate your information. This is just what we've needed to solve several cases."

Greg heaved a sigh of relief. But that still didn't answer the question as to his safety.

Todd finally said, "I need to have you give this testimony so it can be recorded. I would suggest that you quit your job as soon as possible, and move out of that place where you are living. We can set you up in a safe house. Only my partner and I will know where you are."

He said to Joan, "I don't even want you to know so that you can't be targeted." Gulping, Joan agreed. She knew that God's protection was greater than anything the enemy could throw her way.

The two men made the necessary plans for Greg's immediate actions. Following a handshake, hug, and huge thank you, Todd left to get the ball rolling.

Greg smiled at Joan. "How can I thank you? For the first time since I found out what was going on at the warehouse, I have hope. Please keep praying for me. I'm going to need it now more than ever."

Joan and he hugged as she prayed for God's protection for His child. Life certainly was never boring when you serve the Lord!

★ ★ ★

First thing Monday morning, Greg called Scrapper and told him that he was quitting his job.

"What? Why?" asked his supervisor.

"I got an offer I can't refuse," replied Greg.

"So, are you coming back to work this week? You're supposed to give two-week's notice, you know?" asked the angry man.

"Well, this new opportunity starts right away, so I guess I'll just have to forego the two-weeks. Hope that's not going to be a problem," replied Greg.

"Look, Greggie, I could see about giving you a raise if that'll help keep you here. Hate to lose a good worker," offered the desperate man.

"Sorry, Scrapper, but this can't wait. I hope you understand. If you want, tell the other guys 'bye for me, although I doubt that they'll miss me. I'm sure you can find someone else to do the job. I appreciate all your patience with me while I was learning what to do. See ya around," finished Greg.

"Yeah, see ya," replied his former boss as he hung up the phone. Scrapper thought, now what was he going to do? He hated working with Franzoni, but what choice did he have? Maybe he should just leave too as he'd wanted to do. Let the guy figure it out for himself. At least he could go on his own terms, not through actions of others.

★ ★ ★

Within a couple of hours, Greg was sequestered in a nice house in the suburbs.

"I don't know how long you'll have to be here," Todd said, "but let me know if you need anything. We'll be working on the information you gave us as fast as we can. Hopefully, it won't be long before we can wrap this up and you can get on with your life."

"You don't know how much I appreciate this," Greg responded. "For a while I was so scared that I wanted to just run away. But those guys are good and I knew they'd find me. I don't think I left any trail, but you never know. Please be careful. They mean business. Whenever someone gets in their way, he's toast."

"Yeah, we've already figured that out. Don't worry, you're safe here. There's plenty of food in the kitchen, books and TV to keep you occupied. Since you didn't have a car, you won't be traced to here. Just stay inside as much as possible. I know it'll seem almost like prison confinement, but know that you're going to 'get out' soon!" Todd offered.

"Thanks again for everything, Detective. I'm already breathing easier than I have in weeks. Thank God I found Jesus Who will keep me company while I'm here. Please let Joan know that I'm okay. She has come to mean so much to me. How I was ever so blind before is beyond me. I am so grateful for all her, and your, prayers. There aren't words to express my gratitude." Greg couldn't continue without breaking down completely.

"You got it. Anytime you want to send her a message, just give me a call. This won't last long, God willing. See you soon," Todd said, heading to the door.

"Yes, God willing. Thanks again."

"You're welcome."

After Todd left, Greg headed to the comfortable couch in the living room and took a deep breath. Why or how he had been so blessed was still a mystery to him. He knew he didn't deserve any of this, that he couldn't do anything to earn it. "Thank You, Jesus, again for saving me, for protecting me, and for being with me. For the first time in my life, I am not alone or helpless. You've already made such a difference in my life. There aren't enough words to express my thanks."

With that, Greg put his head in his hands and with relief cried like a baby.

CHAPTER 30

The two friends, Joan and Sally, were finishing their lunch as they began their conversation in earnest. You could only say so much while chewing your food!

"So how does it feel to being an almost mother-in-law?" Joan asked her long-time friend.

Sally took a drink of her tea and answered, "You know, I think it will be the best job I've ever had! I couldn't love Gerry any more if she was my own daughter. She is a delightful young woman. Who would have thought all those years ago when she first attended your Sunday school class that she would end up marrying my prodigal son? Of course, the prodigal has come home now, so I guess I can't call him that anymore."

"No, he's definitely not a prodigal any more. You must be so proud of him and all that he's accomplished in his life. Only God could have orchestrated all of that."

"Yes, only God," agreed Sally.

She tucked her napkin under her cleaned plate and then asked Joan, "So what's happening with Greg? You've been rather vague about him lately."

Taking another sip of her water, Joan answered carefully, "As you know, he finally got his life right with God, and I was mentoring him for several weeks; but now he's out of contact again." At her friend's shocked expression, Joan continued. "It's not as bad as it sounds, actually. Because of some information he had to give to the authorities, he's in protective custody so to speak. I can't even make contact with him until it's over."

"Oh, Joan, that must be so hard. Is it dangerous? I mean is his life at stake?"

"As I understand it, it is. Todd Chambers has been keeping me up on Greg's growing faith, and has also told me what he could about the investigation, which isn't much. I'm hoping and praying that this thing is over soon. I'd hate to see Greg relapse into his old life because of it. Todd has assured me that he doesn't think that will happen. One of his friends is mentoring Greg, unaware of his past or the case that necessitated his going into hiding."

"It would seem we need to just keep praying, doesn't it? How does God do it, sorting out all the complications of people's lives? I'm so glad He's God and I'm not!" replied Sally.

"'Boy, that's for sure. I just know that if He can save someone like Greg, then He certainly can keep him safe, and secure in his faith. No one is an impossible case to God."

They went on to talk of other less intense things, filling in each other on their lives and others that they both knew. Joan was still teaching her Sunday school class. Although Sally attended another church, the two friends shared a deep bond. Joan had led Sally to the Lord many years ago after Sally's husband had died suddenly. Even though they didn't see each other that often, they always picked up right where they left off from their last visit. That's what good friends do.

★ ★ ★

A week later, Joan was having lunch with another one of her dear friends, Jenny Chambers. Life had gotten so busy for both of them that carving out time for each other took some doing.

"So, how are you managing now that you've moved into Harriet's house?" Joan asked. "Is it hard to be there without her?"

"We are doing quite well. Actually, we do feel her influence with us quite often. I'm sure she's gazing down on us with satisfaction that we're trying to live up to her expectations. Not that she ever put any pressure on us, but I want to keep her memory alive for as long as possible."

"I'm sure she was already very proud of the wife and mother that you've become. Her gentle strength and faith couldn't help but influence you, as it did so many others."

"She did have a great impact on my life, from many years ago until she passed away. I still can't believe she's gone, even after all this time. But her lessons will always stay with me.

"Because of her generosity, we were able to remodel the house, or at least the kitchen and bathrooms. We redid the roof, painted, and put in new hardwood flooring. We've also enlarged the garage, adding a second parking space, and connected it with the house. It's like a new house, but with the old charm of its era. I love it! We could never have afforded such a huge place otherwise. I still can't believe Harriet was so well off! Who knew?"

Joan just nodded. "I was aware of Harriet's generosity in many other areas and wasn't the least bit surprised to learn of her leaving you her house and finances. You were like the granddaughter she never had, or daughter, as it were. She bragged on you whenever we saw each other."

Nodding, with tears in her eyes, Jenny continued, "Changing the subject, I understand that you've taken over mentoring Janetta and Blanche. How's that going?" Jenny asked her friend.

"Actually, it's going quite well. Harriet did an excellent job of getting them grounded in the Word. I'm more of a sounding board when they need some clarification or another opinion. They have each grown so much in their faith. Your aunt did some good work with them. Just to think that she actually cared more about Janetta's soul than she did about her attempt to steal from her."

Jenny nodded, adding, "Aunt Harriet was definitely one special lady. I don't think she ever met a stranger. There are more people than we can count who will be in heaven because of her faithfulness. What a legacy!"

After a moment's pause, Jenny smiled at her friend, "You will leave quite a legacy yourself. Look at all the people you've influenced over the years: Sally Burnett, and ultimately Randy, Gerry, Lucy, Marie, Peggy, Doris, and so many more, including me. And finally, Greg's conversion is enough to make me want to shout! All your prayers for all of us have amounted to a mountain of changes in our lives. There are not words to thank you for your faithfulness," Jenny said with more tears in her eyes.

Joan swallowed the lump in her throat at Jenny's kind words. With tears in her voice she responded, "I've done nothing for the praise of man, only for the glory of God."

To help lighten the moment, Jenny squeezed her hand and said, "What's for dessert?"

CHAPTER 31

The sun shone brightly, without a cloud in the sky, as Gerry and her parents, John and Mildred, entered Bellwood Community Church. Her dad headed off to get his boutonniere while Gerry and her mom headed to the bridal room.

Carrying her gown in a long zippered bag, Gerry carefully hung it up as soon as she entered the spacious room surrounded with mirrors on three sides. A large screen for privacy was on the fourth wall.

"How lovely," Mildred commented as she surveyed the space.

Gerry replied, "I've always loved this room. It holds so much hope for the future as brides get ready for their walk down the aisle." She couldn't help wondering what it would be like to be married to the love of her life. It didn't seem possible that this day had finally come. Even though she had butterflies tickling her stomach, she knew without a doubt that she was soon to be joined to the man that God had chosen for her. She was more excited than nervous.

Soon, her only attendant, Joan Travis, her matron-of-honor, arrived carrying her dress in a bag. Her mom had come already outfitted in her mother-of-the-bride dress of deep blue.

There was much laughter and a few tears as the women began the transformation.

"Oh Joan, did you ever think that this day would come?" Gerry asked as she slipped into her undergarments behind a screen.

"Yes, I knew it would come but just not when. Haven't we been praying for it for years?" answered Joan.

Gerry agreed but then added, "I'm not sure why it had to take so long. It was probably because Randy was 'otherwise occupied' for much of that time!" They both laughed.

Joan quickly changed into her light blue tea-length dress. It was capped-sleeved, with a square neckline and fitted bodice.

Sally stuck her head in the door, "May I come in?" she asked tentatively.

"Of course, you're a part of this party," Gerry answered.

Sally entered, wearing a medium blue dress similar to the others. "Oh, Gerry, you're like an angel!" They hugged gently trying not to rumple either woman's attire.

"Thank you, Sally. And thank you for raising such a remarkable man. Randy is everything I've ever wanted and more," Gerry said tearfully.

"We can both thank our Savior for that. I only started the ball rolling; He's the One who improved on my model! Actually, I think God made the model, and then rolled the ball back on the right path after it took a detour."

They both laughed and nodded their heads in agreement.

Gerry's dress was simple, also similar but reaching the floor with only a slight train in the back. Lace outlined the neckline and the waistline, with seed pearls scattered throughout.

Soon Gerry stood in the center of the room as Mildred placed her veil on her head and adjusted it around Gerry's shoulders. "You are so lovely, my dear. I can't believe my little girl is getting married."

"I'm not so little anymore," Gerry responded.

"Maybe not, but to me you will always be my little girl, not matter how old you are!" her mom added.

Hugging gently so as to not disturb their dresses, both women blotted tears from their eyes with ever-present tissues. They were happy tears, thankful tears. But aware of all the work put into their makeup, they tried to keep the waterworks from ruining all the effort.

Once everyone was ready, they headed to the empty sanctuary for pictures. The couple had decided to not keep their guests waiting after the ceremony while they were thus occupied. Neither of them believed in bad luck connected with the groom seeing the bride before they tied the knot.

Randy was so handsome in his black suit, white shirt and medium blue tie. As best man, Fred's suit was dark grey, and he also had a white shirt but lighter blue tie.

The photographer put everyone at ease as she directed the next hour of posing and smiling. "Let's have just the bridal party now. Great!" Then it was, "Now we want the bride and groom and their parents. Super!" On and on she went, smiling, making small jokes, and especially helping the guys to relax and act natural and not stiff. She knew her stuff.

Returning to the bridal room, the women enjoyed a light snack. At least those who could eat partook. Gerry's insides were too busy jumping around to make her the least bit hungry. She did have some orange juice for strength.

In less than an hour, there was a knock at the door that told them it was time. The women stood in a circle and Joan offered a prayer for the new couple. Then, gathering her gown around her, Gerry motioned for Sally and her mom to head the procession out of the room.

As each one took her turn walking into the sanctuary, Gerry's dad took her hand and placed it in the crook of his arm. He tried his best not to let the tears escape as he said, "You are so beautiful, my precious daughter. We couldn't be more proud of you." It was all he could say before they both dissolved into tears.

As the wedding processional began and they started down the runner-clad aisle, Gerry looked up to see the wonder on Randy's face. His smile put her at ease as her steps brought her closer to her intended.

Fred Foster, standing with Randy, also had a wide smile on his face. Randy's mother, Sally, was seated on the second row, smiling broadly with glistening eyes. Many of Gerry's students and their families, as well as her fellow teachers, were also there with huge smiles, and a few tears.

When father and daughter reached the altar, John and Randy shook hands before her dad pulled her hand from his arm and placed it in Randy's outstretched palm. He responded to the pastor's, "Who gives this woman to be married to this man?" "Her mother and I," Then he took his seat beside his smiling wife.

Ascending the short stairs to the platform, Gerry handed her bouquet to Joan and they all turned toward the pastor.

"Dearly beloved...." began the pastor. To the young couple, the ceremony took far less time than the rehearsal! Before they knew it he was saying, "Randy, you may kiss your bride."

It didn't take any more encouragement for Randy to pull Gerry into his arms and gently place a kiss of commitment on her lips. She melted into the embrace and returned his caress with her own. The audience began laughing and clapping as the two newlyweds stepped back from their expression of love and faced the congregation, their cheeks tinged in pink.

"Ladies and gentlemen, may I present to you, Mr. & Mrs. Randy Burnett!"

At this the crowd jumped to their feet and began to loudly clap and shout.

Joan handed Gerry her bouquet and the two, who were now one, descended the steps and walked up the aisle with wide grins on their faces.

Joan took Fred's arm as they followed the bridal pair out of the sanctuary.

Once they reached the foyer, the ushers began dismissing the attendees, beginning with Sally and Gerry's parents.

The wedding party retired to a classroom until everyone was seated in the fellowship hall. Since it was not a large wedding, everyone fit in the spacious room.

Then it was time to introduce the wedding party to everyone present.

Again, there were shouts and loud clapping. Instead of a receiving line, Gerry and Randy went around to each table to thank their friends and family for coming, receiving hugs and smiles as they did so.

A light catered luncheon was enjoyed by all. Even though the newlyweds didn't get much time to eat, they did manage a few bites between well-wishers.

When the bouquet was tossed, Janetta Willis caught it, to the delight of Joan and Gerry. Her turn was next!

The cake was cut and enjoyed, toasts were made, and soon it was time for the couple to depart.

Taking her hand, Randy led his bride outside to the waiting rental car amid the bubbles blown by the guests and their shouts of well wishes.

Once settled into their seats, they headed off to their new lives together.

"Where are we going," Gerry asked for the umpteenth time.

"You'll know when we get there," was all her new husband would say.

Relaxing for the first time in weeks, Gerry shut her eyes and let the tears of joy cascade down her cheeks. She didn't think she could be any happier. Silently she thanked God for this incredible man that He had kept for her. There were not words enough to express her gratitude.

★ ★ ★

One short week later, the happy couple pulled up in front of Gerry's house that would now be theirs. Randy had already moved his belongings in before the wedding, and they had spent several hours finding new places for everything, rearranging furniture, etc.

Helping his bride out of the car, Randy took her hand as he led her up the sidewalk. Putting the key in the lock, Randy pushed the door open gently with his foot. He swiftly picked Gerry up and carried her into the living room where he carefully placed her feet on the floor.

"Welcome home, Mrs. Burnett!" he whispered with a huge smile. Looking deeply into each other's eyes, they just stood there, relishing the moment, before ending it with a passionate kiss.

Breaking away reluctantly, Gerry whispered, "Later."

Nodding, Randy returned to the car to bring in their luggage. Taking the bags to the master bedroom, he returned to the living room and it was then he noticed all the wedding gifts waiting to be opened.

"Wow! Are all those for us?" he asked, incredulous.

As Gerry made her way to the couch where most of the bags and packages were piled, she smiled, "It seems that way. Our names are on the cards!"

For the next hour they were like two kids on Christmas morning, oohing and aahing over every one of the gifts, as well as all the gift cards.

"I'm stunned," replied Gerry. She had been writing down each gift and giver for thank you notes later.

Randy added, "Me, too. I never expected to be so blessed with so many wonderful things. I know we put a few things on our wedding registry, but this far exceeds anything we need."

"Isn't that just like our Heavenly Father? He always gives more than we can ask or think," Gerry said, smiling at her new husband. He understood exactly what she meant.

Shortly, most of the gifts had been placed in their new homes in the various rooms where they would be utilized. Only a few were duplicates, and the two of them would decide later what to do about those.

After all of that, Gerry went to the kitchen to find the fixings for dinner. To her great surprise, the refrigerator was well stocked with enough food to fill them up for several days, if not weeks.

"Would you look at this?" she said to her new husband.

"What?" he asked, as he came into the kitchen.

"We have a lot of choices here. I do like to cook, but this is so thoughtful of someone." It was just then that she noticed a piece of paper taped to the refrigerator door.

Reading out loud, she said, "Here's to the happy couple who will probably have more on their minds than cooking, signed, helpful hands."

Eyes on each other, they burst out laughing. Taking his bride in his arms, Randy asked, "Is it later?"

CHAPTER 32

Joan answered her ringing phone, recognizing her son's name in the caller ID.

"Hello, Philip. To what do I owe this mid-day call?" she asked.

"Oh, Mom, Lyle has been kidnapped!!"

"What? How can that be? What happened!" she exclaimed.

Taking a breath, Philip continued, "Penny took Lyle to the park near our house this afternoon so he could work off some of his energy. She was watching him while he played on the swings and slide. There were a couple of other mothers and their children there as well. While talking with one of her friends, a disagreement broke out between two of the children. As she was watching the mothers help to break up the battle, she took her eyes off of Lyle."

"But not for long, right?" Joan inquired.

"No, that's just the thing. It wasn't for more than a few seconds. Lyle had been on the monkey bars near the bushes that are between the park and the street. When she looked up, he was gone. She began calling his name, ran over to the area, and then went through an opening in the bushes to the street. He was nowhere in sight."

"She must have been beside herself! What happened next? Did he just run off with a friend? How can you be sure he was kidnapped?" Joan was praying and talking at the same time.

Philip again took a deep breath. "When she got to the street, a young kid on a bike came up to her and asked if she was trying to find a little boy. He described Lyle perfectly."

Joan interrupted, "Then he knew where he was?"

"Not exactly. He saw a black car with darkened widows pull up to the curb. A guy got out and walked over to the opening in the bushes. He called out a name, but the kid on the bike didn't hear what it was. Soon, a little boy came walking toward the man. They had a short conversation after which the boy hugged the man and followed him to the car. They got in and drove away."

"But that makes no sense. Haven't you told Lyle not to go anywhere with strangers?" Joan was sure that her son and his wife had had that conversation with Lyle on more than one occasion.

"Of course. The boy who saw the whole thing said that Lyle acted like he knew the man. He had a big smile on his face when he got in the car."

"Then who could it have been? Are you sure it wasn't an adult that you already know? Why would he get in a stranger's car and not be frightened?" Joan wanted answers, now!

"I don't know, Mom. The only good thing is that the kid on the bike used his phone to video the whole thing. It seemed a bit fishy to him and he wanted to get as much information as possible in case there were any questions later."

"Oh, thank God! Have the police been notified? Have they found Lyle yet?"

Philip was trying not to choke on his words. "Penny called the police right away. They came and interviewed the boy, and everyone who was in the area. No one else saw a thing. The boy turned his phone over to the officer so that they could review the video. Thanks to his quick thinking, the police should be able to locate the car and, hopefully, our little guy.

"Please pray, Mom. Only God knows where he is and if he is safe."

"Oh, Philip, I'm coming over right now. You know that I'm already praying, and I will alert my church prayer chain. God will return that little guy without a single hair on his head harmed. See you soon."

"Thanks, Mom. I know I can count on you and your friends. Right now, we're both so upset that it's hard to pray intelligently. But God knows our hearts and I'm sure He hears our cries," he said with tears in his voice.

"Of that you can be sure, my dear son. Let's pray right now, okay?"

"Yes, I'd welcome that. My thoughts are so jumbled that it's hard to put together two coherent sentences."

Joan began her prayer for Lyle's safety, then that the culprit would be caught and brought to justice. She also asked for peace and calm to descend on Philip and Penny with the assurance that all would be well.

After she finished, Philip sighed, "Thanks, I needed that! See you soon."

★ ★ ★

As soon as Joan rang the bell, Philip opened the door and drew her into a tight hug. He couldn't help asking, "Why would anyone do this? And why would Lyle be so happy to go with a stranger? Penny is beside herself. She blames herself for not keeping a better eye on Lyle. But how can just a few seconds make such a big difference?"

They stayed that way for quite a few moments before he led her into the living room where Penny was seated. She was wringing her hands and dabbing at her eyes with a soggy tissue.

"Oh Joan, thanks for coming. I don't know what I'll do if something happens to Lyle," she couldn't continue as the tears returned, streaming down her face.

Sitting down beside her, Joan engulfed her in her arms, holding her up as Penny sagged against her. Patting her back, Joan refrained from saying anything at first. She loved this young woman as if she were her own daughter. Hurting for her and Philip, Joan mustered as much strength as she could. She had to be strong for them so they wouldn't fall apart completely.

Having faith in God was one thing, but having to put it to the test like this was another thing altogether. She was certain in her heart of hearts that Lyle would be okay. But it would have to be the loving Savior Who would give them that assurance. Surely He grieved with them.

After several minutes, Penny released her hold on Joan and sat up.

"You have to stay strong," Joan said. "You have another life to think about as well," she indicated the baby that was due in less than two weeks.

"I know, but it's sooo hard! How could Lyle just disappear like that? Who would be so cruel as to take him? Why would he go with someone he didn't know? There are just too many questions and no answers!" Penny was trying her best to hold herself together. Philip was beside her, holding her hand. They both appeared washed out, shaking their heads in disbelief. This just couldn't be happening.

In a few minutes, Joan said, "Let me pray with you. I know the Lord has His eye on Lyle this very minute." With that, she took their hands and lifted everything up to the only One Who could do anything about this terrible situation. Though they felt helpless, He was not.

The waiting and not knowing were the hardest part. Minutes seemed to drag by like days. When would they hear something? Before any of them would let themselves be drawn into the abyss of worry, they tried to comfort one another with assurances of God's faithfulness that they already knew but right now did not feel. Walking by faith and not by sight takes more fortitude than they had ever had to use. Pushing down the horror that wanted to overtake them, and relishing the reunion with Lyle, was what kept them all from dissolving into a heap.

CHAPTER 33

Todd Chambers had just received the information about the kidnapping of Lyle Travis. Realizing that he was Joan Travis's grandson made him want to find that little boy—sooner rather than later. No child or family should be put through that kind of trauma. But Joan was a friend, and he hurt for her.

Praying for the family, and the little boy's safety, he called his partner Kirk to accompany him into the room where the video given to them by Joey Wallings was being set up by the officer who had taken the call.

After viewing the footage, and the information as to the owner of the car, they had hope for the first time since Lyle's disappearance.

As they left the room, Kirk said, "Well, well, well. Do you suppose that we can finally pin something on this guy that will stick?"

Todd replied, "Let's hope so. Shall we make a call on the 'gentleman' in question?"

Todd added, "If only all our cases were this easy." Kirk agreed as they headed for the door, praying that the little boy was unharmed.

★ ★ ★

Soon the two detectives were ringing the bell of the suspect's door.

"Yes?" asked the greeter.

"Are you Gary Travis?" asked Todd, showing his badge. "I'm sure you know why we are here," he added.

"Yes, I have been expecting you, but not quite so soon."

Todd noticed Lyle on the carpet of the spacious condo playing with a toy train set. Thankful that the little guy seemed fine, he turned to their host.

Further questioning found the detectives astounded at the reasoning behind the snatching.

Gary asked, "Is it too much for a grandpa to want to know his grandson? I just wanted to be able to get to know him and give him whatever he wants."

Shaking his head, Todd replied, "You do know that kidnapping is a federal offense? Why didn't you just ask for permission to see him?"

"Don't you think I tried that?" Gary hotly replied. "That ungrateful son of mine didn't want me around or to let me meet that adorable little child. What's a guy to do? I have every right to know him. He's my grandson! That blasted mother of his was probably behind it. She hates my guts with her holier-than-thou attitude. She makes me sick!"

Todd knew that Joan was not at all like her ex's description. What had made this guy so bitter? That was a question that would have to wait until later. Right now he needed to take this guy in and let the courts decide what to do with him, and let Lyle's family know he was safe.

Kirk read the man his rights, while Todd called for back-up to take the man into custody. The well-dressed man didn't put up an argument, although he did seem to become more incoherent with his comments the longer they waited for the officers.

Todd walked over and bent down to talk with Lyle. "Hi there, my name is Todd. I'm a police detective. And who are you?" he asked to put the child at ease.

"I'm Lyle Travis. Look at this great train set my grandpa gave me!"

Todd kept the boy in conversation while the owner of the condo was led away. Rising to his feet, he called Philip Travis.

"Yes," asked an anxious father.

"Philip, this is Detective Chambers."

"Have you found Lyle? Is he okay?" the distraught man begged.

"Yes, we've found him and he's fine," Todd was happy to report.

"Oh, thank You God!" Philip turned to tell Penny and Joan the good news.

Todd continued, "We'll be back at police headquarters shortly. Please meet us there."

"Yes, thank you, thank you. We'll see you soon!" Philip shouted into the phone.

Helping Lyle to pack up his new train, Todd took him by the hand and told him that he was taking him to his daddy and mommy. Lyle grinned as only a trusting child can do, and walked hand-in-hand with the detectives out to their car.

Soon, parents and child experienced a tearful reunion. Lyle was so excited to show his dad and grandma the train set, no worse for wear. Philip, Penny and Joan listened to every word the child spoke, grateful for the quick solution to their distress.

Philip couldn't believe that his own dad had stooped so low as to kidnap Lyle. What had happened to cause Gary to become an entirely different person from the one of his memory?

Joan was shocked at the news about Gary. All these years she had been praying for him. She had tried reasoning with him when she called the number Philip gave her, but he would have none of it. Now to have him do this was unthinkable. Thank God that he hadn't hurt their little boy. Philip may have forgiven Gary for leaving him when he was young, but harming his own son would have been much harder to forgive.

Penny turned to Todd and offered her thanks for finding their son. "Was the video Joey took helpful in locating Lyle?" she asked.

"Oh, yes. The clear picture of the license plate number made our job very easy. Thanks to Joey's quick thinking, we were able to find your son right away."

Philip added, "Is there some public way we can recognize Joey for his actions? We will offer him a reward, but he should be held up as a model of what's good in our young people today."

Todd replied, "I will recommend him to the committee who hands out good citizen awards. I'm sure he will go to the top of their list."

"That's good. Without his help, we might never have...." Philip couldn't finish his sentence. Even though he didn't think Gary would have harmed Lyle, at this point he couldn't be sure of that.

As the happily reunited family left the station, Todd and Kirk set about filling out their reports. Soon Kirk came into Todd's office.

"Well, what do you think? With this action, plus the information we have recently received from Greg Preston, and the others we've questioned, have we finally got enough to send this guy away for a very long time?"

Todd replied with a smile, "I'm sure of it. No high-priced lawyer is going to be able to get him off this time. There's just too much evidence to support the many charges against him. I'm looking forward to seeing him pay for all of his crimes. It's time justice was served."

"I couldn't agree with you more. Thank God that little boy wasn't hurt. Travis was talking so crazy by the time the officers arrived; I was beginning to think he might have to be locked in the psych ward. Maybe he will yet."

"Let's hope that as his sin has found him out, he will have to pay. I can't really feel sorry for the guy. He's done some pretty rotten things over the years if all the information we have is correct. No wonder his mind has started to slip. How can anyone live with himself after that kind of life?"

For several minutes the two detectives pondered the fate of the man in custody. The one called Mr. Big. Todd finally replied, "Why do some people have to turn out to be so corrupted? What made him go from a good citizen to a criminal? Only God can untangle this web of deceit and evil. God have mercy on his soul."

Chapter 34

Not many days later, Joan was enjoying a quiet Sunday afternoon when there was a knock at her door. Opening it she discovered a smiling Janetta Willis and Blanche DuPree.

"Welcome, ladies, please come in," Joan said as she opened the door wider to allow them to enter.

"Mom and I were trying some new recipes and wanted to bring you these cookies for you to try. I hope we're not interrupting anything," offered Janetta.

"Not at all. Why don't you bring those into the kitchen and I'll put on a pot of coffee?" Joan replied leading the way.

Seating themselves at the table while Joan prepared their beverages, Janetta offered, "We don't want to put you out any, we just wanted your opinion on this new recipe."

"No problem at all. I love having company. And those smell delicious. What's in them?"

As the ladies discussed their trials and errors over baking, there was another knock at Joan's door.

"I wonder who that could be?" she said, heading to the living room.

Upon peering through the peephole, she thought, *this could prove interesting.* Opening up the door, she hugged her visitor and followed him into the apartment. "What brings you out on this sunny day? I thought we couldn't have any contact. Has something changed? What's up?" She peppered him with questions.

Greg just smiled and then sighed. "The police have arrested the leader of the pack, so to speak. Unbeknownst to me, he's some big-time crook called Mr. Big they've wanted to find and be able to charge for a long time. My testimony, as well as his most recent escapade, has given them enough ammunition that should get him sent up for a long, long time."

Smiling, Joan replied, "I'm so glad. Now you can get on with your life. Will there be a trial and all that messy stuff before you can do that? How does that work?"

Taking a seat, Greg continued, "It seems the guy kinda went bonkers. He started telling the police all about his past actions without so much as a question from them. It was as if he was glad to finally get it all off his chest."

"He didn't consult his lawyer first?"

"No, he just confessed to a whole bunch of stuff, as I understand it, even a few murders, along with the smuggling. Poor guy, I almost feel sorry for him, almost."

Greg added, "All of his 'organization' has also been arrested, even the guys I worked with. Some of them knew a lot more than they ever let on. More than one of them had been skimming off the top for themselves for a long time. I'm so glad I didn't get caught up in that. There's no telling where I'd be now."

"Wow, that's unbelievable, what God has done!"

"Yeah, you could say that. The only thing is, this guy is someone you know, or used to know."

Stunned, Joan looked at Greg with question marks all over her face. "Someone I know? How can that be?" Seeing Greg's face, she didn't like where this conversation was going.

"I hate to be the bearer of such bad news, but the guy is Gary Travis, your ex-husband," Greg replied quietly.

Falling into the nearest chair, Joan couldn't believe what she had just heard. "Gary? How can that be? He was such a kind, loving man. Although the last time I saw him, he wasn't so kind. What happened to him?"

Just then, Joan's other two guests walked into the living room. Janetta saw Greg and gasped. "Greg? Is that you? What are you doing here?"

"Janetta? I could ask you the same thing," replied the astonished young man.

Just as they were getting settled, another knock came to Joan's door. "It's getting to be like Grand Central around here!"

Opening the door to Todd Chambers, Joan just reached up and gave him a big hug with tears in her eyes. He wondered how she knew about Gary until he saw Greg seated on the couch.

"Well, it's like old home week," he commented.

"Please join us. There's still a bit of coffee, and some delicious cookies. You remember Janetta and her mother, Blanche?"

"Of course, how are you ladies?" Todd said, grabbing a cookie and then pulling a chair up from the desk in the corner.

After pleasantries were exchanged, he acknowledged Joan. "I suppose Greg has already told you about Gary?"

"Yes, what a shock! I can't believe he'd do any of the things he's admitted."

"It seems it was the last straw for him when you and Philip didn't want him to meet his grandson. From what he ranted on about after his arrest, he didn't like being told 'no' by anyone. Did you know that he had a twin sister who died when he was young?"

"No. He never mentioned her at all," said a curious Joan.

"Apparently, his sister Jolene was born with a genetic disease that required all of his parents' time. And for some reason, they blamed him for her disabilities—for being normal. Not only that, they were extremely religious but rigid people who showed him little affection. They constantly told him to stay out of their way, never letting him get close to or help with his sister.

"After she died, they pulled away emotionally from him even more. He couldn't wait to go to college, never returning home to see his parents. He cut off all contact with them. In school he was able to push himself to become a leader, not a follower. He soon found out that a happy-go-lucky personality got him a long way."

Joan murmured, "Gary always seemed content, outgoing and fun. Why did he change?"

Todd continued, "After your daughter died, he was sure you were going to act just like the parents he had fled. He couldn't take it when you began to reexamine your faith. It was the last straw as far as he was concerned.

"For some crazy reason, he justified everything he's done, and the power he's wielded over others. No one had stood up to him without dire consequences. He wasn't about to let either of you get the better of him either, or so he thought. He couldn't bring himself to harm you physically, but decided taking Lyle would 'teach you both a lesson,' whatever that meant."

Joan just sat there, stunned. She had always thought that they parted on good terms all those years ago. Gary may not have been the best father, but he was never cruel. She couldn't imagine what had turned him into what now seemed like a monster. She didn't even want to know all the details. Only God could sort it all out.

Turning to Blanche, Todd said, "I don't know if you were ever told this, but Jake Willis, your ex-husband, aka Roberto Jenks, was killed last year. It was by order of Mr. Big—Gary Travis."

Janetta and Blanche acknowledged his words without so as much as a tear in their eyes.

"We lost contact with him a very long time ago. I'm sorry he was killed; but with the kind of life he was living, it doesn't surprise me," commented Blanche, quietly.

"Too bad he never had the chance to meet Jesus," commented Janetta.

Greg looked up at her with shock on his face.

"You're a Christian?" he asked.

"Oh yes. Remember that dear old lady who was the object of our phone scam? She came to see me while I was locked up and led me to my Savior. I'll forever be grateful for the love and care she bestowed on me. And once Mom found out where I was, we renewed our relationship. Soon she was also a believer," she said.

Greg turned to Joan. "It's true," she replied. "Harriet Reynolds led Janetta to the Lord, Janetta led her mom to Him, and then Harriet mentored them until she died a few months ago at ninety. Now, I try to fill in for her as best I can."

"Praise God!" Greg shouted.

Janetta just smiled.

Printed in the United States
By Bookmasters